JUMPING JENNY

JUMPING JENNY

BONNIE PRYOR

ILLUSTRATED BY ANITA RIGGIO

MORROW JUNIOR BOOKS
NEW YORK

To the real Jenny,
who brings laughter and love

Inquiries should be addressed to
William Morrow and Company, Inc.,
1350 Avenue of the Americas, New York, N.Y. 10019.

Printed in the United States of America.

1 2 3 4 5 6 7 8 9 10

Library of Congress Cataloging-in-Publication Data
Pryor, Bonnie
Jumping Jenny / Bonnie Pryor; illustrated by Anita Riggio.
p. cm.
Summary: The year that Jenny starts kindergarten, she has a busy
time in the classroom and at home trying to adjust to some grown-up changes.
ISBN 0-688-09684-0
[1. Family life—Fiction. 2. Sisters—Fiction. 3. Kindergarten—
Fiction. 4. Schools—Fiction.] 1. Riggio, Anita, ill.
II. Title.
PZ7.P94965Ju 1992
[Fic]—dc20 91-39979 CIP AC

Contents

— 1 —

Glad Jenny

"I'm flying," Jenny shouted to her mother as she pumped the swing higher and higher. Her mother looked up from where she was reading in the shade of the back porch and waved. "Look, Mama," Jenny called again. "I'm a bird."

Mrs. Bingham smiled at her younger daughter. "Be careful," she warned. "You're awfully high."

Jenny was not the kind of girl who liked being careful, but she did let the swing slow down a little to please her mother. As it slowed, she bent her head back to look at the sky. For a second the world seemed to swirl, and her stomach did a strange-feeling flip-flop. "I *like* to be high," she called down to her mother. Now the whole world looked upside down. She could see the family cat sitting by the edge of the porch. Ginger seemed to be dozing, but Jenny knew she was really watching a fat robin a few feet away, by the fence. Since Jenny was looking at it upside down, the bird seemed to be bouncing on its head as it pecked at something hidden in the grass.

"No," shouted Jenny as Ginger got up slowly, ready to pounce. But she needn't have worried. The little bell Mrs. Bingham had hooked to her collar tinkled merrily, and the robin escaped just in time. Ginger sat back down with a disappointed look.

Mrs. Bingham closed the big, thick book. "I'm going to make lunch," she called. "Would you like a tuna sandwich?"

The swing slowly came to a stop, and Jenny held tightly to the ropes until the dizzy feeling passed. "Peanut butter," she said firmly.

Her mother laughed. "You will only be in school half a day this year, so you will eat lunch at home. But it will be easy to make your lunches when you get to first grade. Peanut butter is all you ever want."

"Sometimes I like spaghetti," Jenny reminded her.

"I don't think spaghetti would go very well in a lunch box," Mrs. Bingham said.

Jenny did not want to think about school on such a lovely summer day. Part of her felt happy and excited when she thought about going to kindergarten. Then she'd get that same funny feeling in her stomach as when she swung upside down, but not nearly so pleasant.

The inside of the house was a cool relief from the muggy, late-August heat of Ohio. Mrs. Bingham let Jenny make her own peanut butter sandwich while she fixed herself some tuna fish and poured them both a glass of milk.

Jenny looked inside her mother's book to see if she knew any of the words. But the print was very tiny, and all the words seemed very long. There were a lot of pictures of skeleton bones. Mrs. Bingham read to Jenny every night before bed, but this didn't look like the kind of story she would like to hear.

"Is this a scary book?" asked Jenny.

"No, it's a book about your body," Mrs. Bingham replied. "It's one of my old nursing textbooks. I'm just brushing up."

Jenny looked at her mother. Brushing up with a book seemed a very curious thing to do. How could a person brush up with a book? She tried to imagine her mother brushing her hair with a big, heavy book. It made a funny picture in her head. Then she thought about her mother brushing her teeth with a book instead of a toothbrush.

The telephone rang before Jenny had a chance to ask her mother what she meant. While her mother chatted on the phone, Jenny broke off a piece of her sandwich and fed it to Lady, the family collie. Lady was not allowed to beg food from the table, but she liked to sit under Jenny's chair, waiting for a crumb or two to fall on the floor.

Jenny liked to watch how Lady chewed the peanut butter when it stuck to the roof of her mouth. Lady loved people food. She would eat anything Jenny gave her except lettuce, which Jenny didn't much like herself. Ginger was a fussy eater like Jenny. She would not eat peanut butter. Once Jenny had offered her some, but Ginger had only sniffed at it and walked away with a yawn.

Mrs. Bingham finished her conversation and came back in the room in time to see Lady still smacking her lips over the tasty treat.

"Can I wash the dishes?" Jenny asked quickly before her mother could scold her for giving part of her lunch to the dog.

"May I?" Mrs. Bingham corrected automatically. She squeezed some soap into the sink and ran some water while Jenny carried the plates and glasses from the table, proud to be helping. Her nine-year-old sister, Abigail, was usually given the job of washing dishes, but today she was visiting a friend down the street. Abigail did not like to wash dishes. She complained that the water made her hands wrinkle and that washing dishes was the most boring job in the world. Jenny's job was dusting the furniture, and she thought that was a much more boring job. She didn't know why their mother wouldn't let them change jobs. She loved to get her hands in the soft soap bubbles.

"Be sure to rinse them carefully," Mrs. Bingham instructed. She filled a large pitcher with water at the tap and went to water the houseplants. Mrs. Bingham's hobby was raising houseplants, and Mr. Bingham sometimes complained that he was living in a jungle. He told people that his wife had a green thumb. Jenny often looked at her mother's thumbs, but they never looked green to her. It was another one of those funny things that grown-ups often said.

Jenny climbed up on the sturdy kitchen step stool. She scrubbed each dish and rinsed it carefully. Some of the water splashed on the front of her shirt and in a little puddle on the floor, but

the dishes looked shiny and clean. Jenny could even see her face in them, just like in the commercial on TV. The girl on TV had fluffy hair, and she burst out in song when she saw the clean dishes.

"Sparkle, sparkle, dishes so bright," Jenny sang loudly, imagining she was that girl.

"It looks like you washed yourself along with the dishes," Mrs. Bingham said good-naturedly when she returned to the kitchen. She admired Jenny's work. "These are the cleanest dishes I ever saw," Mrs. Bingham said, just as Abigail walked in the back door.

Jenny could not resist a triumphant smirk at her sister.

"Why don't you let her wash all the dishes?" Abigail said. She gave Jenny a mean look behind her mother's back and stuck out her tongue.

"Quit making faces at me," Jenny said. This was not exactly tattling in Jenny's mind, since she had spoken to her sister and not to her mother.

"Both of you can quit making faces." Mrs. Bingham had heard this argument before. Jenny wondered how her mother knew she had made a face, too, since Mrs. Bingham hadn't even turned around. Perhaps it was true, as she had once heard someone say, that mothers had eyes in the backs of their heads. She tried to imagine two tiny eyes hidden under her mother's dark, curly hair. That gave her an idea for a picture to draw. She jumped down from the little stool she had stood on to wash dishes and ran to her room.

"Jenny must be going to draw another one of her dumb pictures," she heard Abigail say.

Abigail was a little jealous of Jenny's drawing. She did not understand that sometimes Jenny had pictures in her head that she had to put on paper for everyone to see. The whole front of the Binghams' refrigerator was covered with Jenny's pictures, held on with little magnets. More than anything, Jenny liked to draw. She thought she might like to be an artist when she grew up. She hoped her new teacher, Mrs. Archer, would allow lots of time for drawing pictures.

Jenny was starting kindergarten the next week. Mrs. Bingham had already taken her for a visit to the kindergarten room, so that Jenny could see what it was like. Jenny had been pleased to see little cups of paint and trays of crayons lined up neatly on a table at the back of the room.

Her picture was almost finished when Ginger

jumped right up on the little table. "You silly old cat," Jenny scolded. She tried to sound ferocious, but Ginger was not fooled. A rumbly purr sounded deep in her throat, and she settled herself comfortably on the pile of Jenny's drawings.

"Will you miss me while I'm at school?" Jenny scratched behind Ginger's ear in her favorite place. Then she buried her face in the cat's thick, soft fur. "I'm going to miss you."

— 2 —

Mad Jenny

The next day began with gray clouds and drizzly, gloomy rain. At breakfast Jenny discovered that her mother had forgotten to buy her favorite cereal. While she was complaining about it, her cornflakes got soggy. Then, when she pushed her bowl away, she pushed too hard, and the whole bowl fell upside down on the floor. Jenny was sent to the uncooperative chair to think over her behavior.

To make her even more miserable, Abigail had found ways to walk by the uncooperative chair three times, each time with a smile on her face that was more like a smirk. "Abby's making faces at me," Jenny screamed. But, instead of scolding Abigail, Mrs. Bingham made Jenny turn the chair to the wall.

A day like that could only get worse, and just

before dinner, Jenny was banished to her room. She scrunched up her face into the meanest look she could manage and looked in the mirror, pleased with the results. "I am mad," she said out loud. "Mad, mad, *mad.*"

She took some paper and a black crayon from her desk drawer and drew a picture of her mother. She made an ugly face with a turned-down mouth, and she added little sharp horns on her mother's head to give her an extra mean look. Jenny looked at her creation. Then, nodding to herself, she carefully wrote a word underneath. Up, down, up, down for an *M. A*—that was easy. But she had to say the word to herself to figure out the last letter. *D,* that was it. Jenny made a big, fat *D* and held the paper up to admire her work. The picture looked so funny, Jenny almost giggled. But she made another mean face in the mirror to remind herself that she was still angry.

She could hear Abigail downstairs practicing her piano lesson. Mrs. Bingham was humming along as she started preparing dinner. No one seemed very sorry that Jenny was alone in her room.

Jenny knew that her mother would not appreciate being turned into a monster, even on paper. She took the picture and stuffed it in her drawer behind her socks.

She opened her door a tiny crack. "May I come out of my room yet?" she called.

"Are you sorry?" asked Mrs. Bingham from the bottom of the stairs.

"No!" Jenny answered honestly.

"Then stay in your room and think about it some more," said Mrs. Bingham.

Jenny shut the door hard enough to let her mother know she was angry, but not hard enough to get into more trouble. She sat down on her bed to think. All she had done was bounce Ginger on the bed. Jenny liked to bounce. Sometimes her father held her in his upstretched arms before he tucked her in at night. "One for the money. Two for the show. Three to get ready, and four to go," he would sing. On the count of four, Mr. Bingham would drop her down on the bed. Just for a second it would feel like flying. Then she would land on the bed with a big bounce. Jenny loved it. She loved any kind of bouncing. Even when she walked, she liked to skip. That was why her father called her Jumping Jenny. And that was why she had bounced Ginger on the bed. She wanted Ginger to know how much fun it was.

It was true that Ginger hadn't acted like she thought it was fun. The first time, she had jumped off the bed and hidden in the corner. But Jenny had decided it was because she was surprised. So she had tried it again. And again. That was when Ginger had made the loud *meeeoww* sound that made Jenny's mother come running to see if she was hurt. Mrs. Bingham had been very upset. "Animals depend on us to protect them and be kind to them," she had scolded.

"I *was* being kind," Jenny had protested. "I was teaching her how to have fun."

That's when Jenny was told to stay in her room.

Jenny thought about Ginger. Everyone in the Bingham family loved their cat, who had been born on the same day as Abigail. Ginger was lazy and fat, but she loved all the Bingham family, too. Each day she allowed each one of them to hold her, moving from lap to lap, so no one felt slighted.

But what if Ginger didn't like Jenny anymore? What if she sat in everyone else's lap and ran away when she saw Jenny? Suddenly tears rolled down Jenny's cheeks, and she choked out big, noisy sobs.

"My goodness, what's the matter?" Mrs. Bingham asked, opening the door.

"I just wanted Ginger to have some fun," Jenny cried. "And now she won't like me anymore."

Mrs. Bingham sat on the bed next to Jenny. "I think if you talk very quietly and gently to Ginger, she will forgive you. You are getting to be a big girl. You have to learn to think before you do things."

Jenny rested her head on her mother's shoulder. "I don't want to be big. I'd like to stay little so I can stay home with you." She looked at her mother's face. "What will you do all day when I'm gone?"

"I've been thinking about going back to school myself," admitted Mrs. Bingham. "It might be kind of lonesome around here with both my girls gone. I could be busy in school, learning new things and making new friends just like you."

"What if I don't make any friends?" asked Jenny. "What if no one likes me?"

"They will," Mrs. Bingham said, giving her a loving squeeze. "You made friends in preschool, didn't you? And you have friends at Sunday school. It will be kind of like that, only better. You know how you've been starting to learn how to read? Mrs. Archer will help you with that, and you'll learn other new things, too."

"I'd like to have a best friend, like Abby has," Jenny told her mother.

"Best friends are a little harder to find," Mrs. Bingham said with a smile. "But I'm sure you'll find one soon."

"Abigail has two best friends," said Jenny. "That's not fair for her to have two when I don't have any."

"You have friends," Mrs. Bingham said. "What about Sarah and Paul?"

Mrs. Bingham was friendly with Sarah and Paul's mother, and they often came to visit. But the only thing Sarah ever wanted to do was sit and play dolls. Jenny did not mind a few minutes of sitting quietly, but not all afternoon. Paul was a lively little boy, but he was only four. Jenny knew exactly the kind of best friend she wanted. Her best friend should be almost six, just like Jenny. She would be a person who was not afraid to climb trees and who liked to tell secrets.

Abigail was allowed to walk a block away to visit her friends Rachel and Pam, who lived next door to each other. Sometimes the girls came to visit. They went to Abigail's room and shut the door. When Jenny knocked, her sister yelled things like "Scram" or "Get lost." Jenny knew that when she found a best friend, they would play in her room and never let Abigail in, no matter how much she begged.

Mrs. Bingham let Jenny come downstairs with her. She went back to preparing dinner, and Jenny went to the living room to wait for her father to come home from work. Mr. Bingham was an accountant. Jenny knew that meant he worked a lot with numbers. Jenny was not very interested in numbers. She was very interested in reading. She had asked her mother and father to read her favorite books to her so often that she could recite every word in them by heart.

Jenny sat on the couch and watched out the window for her father. She was determined to be the best-behaved child in the whole world, at least for the rest of the day. "I am being very good," she told herself over and over.

Ginger strolled into the room. Ordinarily, she would have run right over to the couch and jumped on Jenny's lap. But now her ears were flattened back, and her eyes looked like tiny slits.

Jenny got down from the couch and crawled across the floor very slowly. "I'm sorry, Ginger," she crooned. "I'm sorry I bounced you." Very gently, she reached out and stroked Ginger's soft fur.

Ginger seemed about to spring away, but after a minute, she relaxed and rolled over on her back, allowing Jenny to scratch her stomach. Seeing Ginger upside down gave Jenny an idea.

"Look, Ginger," she said. "I can stand on my head." She put her head down and gave her legs a push up. But she pushed too hard and fell over with a lopsided plop. She tried three more times, but as soon as she managed to get her legs up, she fell over again. Ginger jumped up on the back of a chair, a safe distance away.

Jenny had imagined the surprised look on her father's face if he came in and saw her standing on her head. She looked around for something to help her stay up. Then she had an idea. Maybe she could do her headstand against the wall. That way, her feet couldn't fall over.

The coat closet door was across the hall from the front door, and next to it was a little table that held her mother's giant fern plant. If she stood on her head against the closet door, she would be the first thing Mr. Bingham would see when he came in. Smiling to herself at her good idea, Jenny put her head as close to the closet door as she could and slowly raised her feet. It worked! The hard floor made her head hurt just a little, but everything in the room had turned upside down.

Lady walked into the hallway. She didn't seem to find it strange to see Jenny's face where her feet should be. She walked over and gave her a big, slurpy lick right on her face.

Several things happened at once. "Yuck, dog germs," Jenny yelled. Suddenly she tottered and started to fall sideways toward her mother's beautiful fern. It still might have been all right, except at that precise minute, Mr. Bingham opened the door and stepped inside. A second later, the fern, Lady, Jenny, and Mr. Bingham were all in a tangled-up heap on the floor.

After dinner Jenny sat on the couch, petting Lady. Mrs. Bingham's fern had been repotted, although many of the fronds were twisted and bent. Mr. Bingham had managed to repair the little table. But her parents were not very happy with her. They were in the kitchen this very minute, discussing the problem.

Jenny had tried to listen. Before the door had been firmly shut, she had heard her father say "rambunctious." She rather liked the sound of

that word, even though she was not quite sure what it meant.

"Daddy says I'm rambunctious," she told Abigail, rolling the word slowly off her tongue. It sounded bouncy to her ears.

"You'd better get Lady off the couch before Mama sees her," Abigail warned.

For the first time Jenny really noticed the dog beside her. "Lady," she exclaimed. Lady jumped down with a mournful look, which said plainly that she thought rules about staying off couches were very unfair to dogs.

"Do you want to play house?" Jenny asked hopefully.

"Not right now," answered Abigail. "I've got to finish this book."

"Will you read it to me?" Jenny asked next.

"It's too old for you," Abigail said. She settled in the chair and opened the book. There was a big black horse on the cover, rearing wildly on his back legs. Abigail loved horses. Her bedroom shelves were full of horse statues, and almost every book she read was about them, too.

"Mama says I'm getting big," said Jenny.

"Not big enough for this. It would just be boring to you."

Jenny leaned over the back of the chair. "What's that word?" she said, pointing to the heading at the top of the page.

"Black," Abigail answered absently.

"I know how to spell *red,"* Jenny said. "R-e-d."

"Terrific. Now beat it. I want to finish this. I'm at the most exciting part," said Abigail.

"You said it was boring," Jenny reminded her.

"To you, not to me," answered Abigail.

Jenny thought about that for a while. Then she leaned over the chair. "What's that word?"

Abigail slammed her book down. *"Stallion,"* she shouted. "Why are you such a pest?"

"I'm not a pest," Jenny explained patiently. "I'm rambunctious."

Abigail went to the closet and pulled out her jacket just as their parents came out of the kitchen.

"Where are you going?" Jenny asked suspiciously.

"Pam is stopping by. We're going to walk to the library," Abigail answered.

"Can I go, too?" Jenny asked.

"Not this time," Mr. Bingham said. He sat down in the comfortable easy chair.

"I want to go, too," Jenny whined. She stamped her foot on the floor.

"You are not big enough to walk that far," her father answered.

"When will I be big enough?" Jenny demanded.

"When we see signs that you are growing up," Mrs. Bingham answered.

Grown-ups certainly said strange things sometimes, thought Jenny. She pictured herself with little "growing up" signs stuck all over her. "What signs?" Jenny asked.

"Like not stamping your feet when you don't get your own way," replied Mrs. Bingham. She sat down on the couch beside Jenny. "Daddy and I have been talking. Do you remember when Abby took swimming lessons at the youth center? A beginner class for gymnastics is starting there soon. We thought we might register you if you're interested."

"Then you could really learn how to stand on your head," Mr. Bingham added.

Jenny forgot all about her earlier mishap. She jumped up and twirled around. "I would love to do that," she exclaimed. "I already know how to do some gymnastics." She pronounced the word carefully. Before anyone could say a word to stop her, she flipped across the floor in a perfect cartwheel. But the room was not wide enough for such a trick, and she crashed into the wall.

"Jenny," shouted Mr. Bingham. "We don't do cartwheels in the house." Seeing the tears in her eyes, he asked in a kinder voice, "Are you all right?"

"I bumped my elbow," Jenny sobbed.

Abigail rolled her eyes. "Why does she get gymnastics lessons and not me?" she asked in a sulky voice.

"Because you take piano lessons now. That's all we can afford," Mrs. Bingham answered.

Abigail still looked grumpy. Jenny rubbed her sore elbow and sniffed back the tears. "I could teach Abby gymnastics when I get home each time," she offered generously.

"I think that's a great idea," said Mrs. Bingham. "As long as it's not in the house."

Abigail looked brighter. "Then I could teach you some piano."

"Good," said Mr. Bingham. "That's a very grown-up compromise."

"Is that one of those signs?" Jenny asked.

"I guess it is." Mrs. Bingham smiled.

"Then can I go to the library?"

"No," said both of the Binghams together.

— 3 —

Colds and Crayons

That Saturday Mrs. Bingham woke up sick. "I have a terrible cold," she said. Only it sounded like "I hab a terrible code."

"You stay in bed, dear," said Mr. Bingham. "I'll fix breakfast and take Abigail to her piano lesson."

After breakfast Jenny curled up in the big chair in the living room. "Do I have to go?" she asked her dad. "I could stay here and watch cartoons."

"All right," Mr. Bingham said. "You can take care of Mama until I get back."

Jenny waved as her father pulled out of the driveway. Then she sat down and turned the dial through all the television stations. Nothing looked very interesting. The house seemed empty and much too quiet.

"We'd better go check on Mama," Jenny told Lady. Together they padded upstairs and down the hall to her mother's bedroom, and Jenny listened outside the door. She could hear Mrs. Bingham's raspy breathing. As quietly as a mouse, Jenny opened the door.

Mama was bundled in the covers with her eyes closed. Jenny came a little closer. She leaned over the bed, trying to see if her mother was awake. Then Lady gave Mrs. Bingham a big, slurpy kiss right on her cheek.

Mrs. Bingham sat straight up and shrieked something that sounded like "Wad was dat?" Then she saw Lady and wiped her cheek.

"I was worried about you," Jenny explained. "It was awfully quiet."

Mrs. Bingham blew her nose. "You better not get too close," she said. "You might get my germs."

"I don't have anything to do," Jenny complained. "Could I stay in here with you? I'll read you a story," she suggested. She ran to her bedroom and returned with her favorite book.

Mrs. Bingham pointed to the soft easy chair in the corner. "Sit there," she suggested. "We'll have a little girl talk."

Ginger was already curled up in the chair. She

did not seem very happy to share her warm napping spot. But Jenny stroked her until she settled back down with a contended purr.

"Cats have awfully boring lives, don't they?" Jenny said. "All they do is eat and sleep."

"I don't suppose it's boring to a cat." Mrs. Bingham propped herself up on some pillows and blew her nose again. "Ginger likes to chase a string sometimes."

"And to crawl inside of grocery sacks," Jenny added. "Maybe that's exciting to a cat." She thought for a minute and then said, "I'm glad I'm a people. Otherwise, I wouldn't be able to take gymnastics lessons."

"Daddy is going to stop at the youth center while Abigail's taking her piano lesson and get you registered."

"I'll bet I'm the best one in the class," Jenny said. "I already know how to do a somersault and a cartwheel."

"There will be a lot of other children," Mrs. Bingham cautioned her. "Some of them might be pretty good, too."

But Jenny was already picturing herself on television, with crowds of people roaring approval as she flipped lightly over the gymnastics mat.

Mrs. Bingham pulled another tissue from the box. "We're all going to be learning new things. Remember I told you I was thinking about going back to school?" Mrs. Bingham asked. "Well, I'm all set. I'm going to take a morning class three days a week. That means I'll have to be leaving the house before breakfast. On Thursdays I'll spend the afternoon in a science lab."

Jenny was so startled she forgot to ask what a science lab was. She did remember her mother mentioning something about school. But she had not really paid attention. Now she laughed. "You already went to school."

"Before you were born, I was a nurse. But it's been so long, I need to take a few refresher courses. Now that both of you girls will be in school every day, I might return to nursing."

"Will I have to have a baby-sitter?" Jenny frowned.

Mrs. Bingham grabbed another tissue and sneezed four times. "Some of Daddy's accounting work can be done at home. So Daddy has decided to fix up an office space in the den. That way, he'll be here on the days when I'm in school. But it's going to mean some big adjustments for all of us."

"Does Daddy know how to fix French toast?" Jenny asked.

Mrs. Bingham nodded. "I think he could do that."

"Tell him I like lots of syrup," Jenny said.

"I'll tell him." Mrs. Bingham gave her a tired smile. "Now, why don't you go draw me a picture, while I take a little nap. Daddy should be home pretty soon."

Jenny skipped downstairs to the living room. But she had forgotten to get crayons and paper from her room. She raced back up to her bedroom and scooped up her drawing supplies. Back to the living room she skipped, this time with her arms full. Then suddenly, she crashed right into the coffee table.

"Ohhh," Jenny yelled loudly. She sat on the floor, holding her knee where she'd bumped it on the sharp edge of the table.

Her mother came running from her room, wrapping her robe around her as she ran.

"I think I broke my knee." Jenny wailed even louder.

Mrs. Bingham inspected her knee. "You'll probably have a pretty good bruise, but it's not broken," she said comfortingly. She gave Jenny a cloth wrapped around some ice.

"Sit in the chair and hold this on your knee for a few minutes," said Mrs. Bingham. "It will make it feel better."

Mrs. Bingham went back upstairs to bed. Jenny held the ice on her knee, feeling very sorry for herself. She had only hurt her knee because she been hurrying to make Mama a picture. And now Mama didn't even seem sorry. Daddy was certainly going to be upset that Mama had let her sit all by herself with a broken knee.

The ice did make her knee feel better. Jenny could never be unhappy for very long. Her crayons were still on the floor where she had dropped them. Lady curled up beside her while she started to draw. She decided to make a picture of herself with curly hair, wearing a beautiful golden dress.

"There," she said finally, holding the picture up for Lady to admire. But as Lady sniffed at the paper, a piece of gold crayon fell out of her mouth. "Bad dog," Jenny scolded. She looked everywhere for her favorite crayon. But the little chewed stub was all she could find. Jenny pried Lady's mouth open and looked inside. There were gold specks on Lady's teeth.

A little worry popped into Jenny's head. She

thought about all that crayon in Lady's stomach. Maybe it would make her sick. Maybe it would even make her die. Jenny felt completely miserable. She didn't want to bother her mother again. Daddy had asked her to take care of Mama. But it wasn't fair of Daddy to expect her to take care of things. Didn't he know she was too little? What if Daddy expected her to take care of things when Mama went back to school? Maybe she would even have to make her own French toast. Big tears welled up in Jenny's eyes. She began to sob as loudly as she could.

Once again Mrs. Bingham came rushing downstairs.

"What is the matter now?" she asked. "Does your knee hurt that much?"

Shaking her head, Jenny pointed to Lady. "Lady's going to get awfully sick. She might even die."

Through her tears, she explained about the crayons.

Mrs. Bingham took a clean tissue from her pocket and wiped Jenny's tears. "I don't think the crayon will hurt her," she said. "Dogs have pretty tough stomachs."

"You mean it's going to stay in her stomach forever?"

Mrs. Bingham laughed. "No. It will probably come out when she does her business."

Jenny understood what her mother meant. Still, a picture of Lady sitting at a desk in one of her father's business suits popped into her head and she giggled. Then she snuggled close to her mother. "I think you had better stay home and take care of things," she said.

Mrs. Bingham put her arms around Jenny. "All these changes do sound a little scary, don't they? But families change and grow all the time. That's what makes life interesting. As long as we love each other and help each other, we'll be all right."

When Mr. Bingham and Abigail came home a few minutes later, they were surprised to see Mrs. Bingham sitting in a chair with Jenny, watching cartoons.

"Guess what, Daddy," Jenny said cheerfully. "Mama says you'll fix me French toast whenever I want." Before Mr. Bingham could reply, she added, "Mama feels much better. But I broke my knee and Lady's going to have gold sparkles in her business." Then she grinned at her mother. "I think life is getting more interesting already."

— 4 —

Looking for God

The first Sunday in September, a warm sun beamed down from a clear blue sky. The weather man reported that the afternoon would be warm. Mrs. Bingham was still blowing her nose, but she was feeling well enough to attend church with the rest of the family.

Jenny liked Sunday school, but she was unusually quiet all the way home. "Change your clothes," Mrs. Bingham said as they walked into the house. "I'm going to fix us a little dinner. It's such a lovely day; maybe we can have one last picnic at the park before school starts."

"Oh, good," squealed Abigail. "Can we go to the duck pond?"

New Albany, Ohio, was a small town, but there was a lovely park nearby. Once it had been only a few weedy acres with a muddy pond. But Mayor Snodgrass had organized a clean-up day, and almost everyone in the town had come to plant flowers, mow, and install playground equipment. Soon the wild ducks had discovered the pond. And then someone donated a flock of domestic ducks. Now the park was everyone's favorite place to picnic.

"Sounds good to me," said Mr. Bingham. With four very different personalities in the house, the Binghams sometimes had difficulty agreeing on places to go. But today the family's mood seemed to match the weather. When everyone was happy like this, Jenny felt like she was in the middle of a giant hug, all warm and cozy. Still, her thoughtful mood continued as she and Abigail went upstairs to change. She was thinking about something her Sunday school teacher had told her.

Mrs. Bingham was mixing the potato salad when she heard a strange noise from upstairs. It sounded like it was coming from the bathroom. BUMP! BUMP! BUMP!

"What on earth is that?" Mrs. Bingham asked her husband.

"I'll go check," said Mr. Bingham, looking as

puzzled as his wife. He went to the closed bathroom door and called, "Jenny. What on earth are you doing?"

BUMP! BUMP!

"Jenny Bingham," Mr. Bingham said sternly. "What are you doing?"

Jenny yanked open the door. Her face was scrunched up in a scowl. "My Sunday school teacher lied," she said.

"What are you talking about?" Mr. Bingham looked very confused.

"My Sunday school teacher said that God was everywhere," Jenny said. "But I can't see Him. So I thought I could trap Him in the shower because I can shut the door real quick. But watch this!"

With that, she slid the shower door open as fast as she could. BUMP! "See?" she said.

Mr. Bingham still looked confused.

"He's not there," Jenny shouted. Tears of frustration sprang into her eyes. "I wanted to say hello and thank Him for this nice picnic day."

"Oh, I see," said Mr. Bingham. "I think your Sunday school teacher is right. God is everywhere. But maybe a bathroom isn't the right place to look for Him. Let's try somewhere else."

Jenny and her father headed out the kitchen

door. "Where are you two going?" asked Mrs. Bingham. "I have our picnic almost ready."

"We're going out to look for God," Jenny called back cheerfully.

Abigail almost dropped the bowl of potato salad she was packing in the picnic basket, and even Mrs. Bingham looked startled. But Jenny and her father didn't stop to explain. Jenny smiled inside herself. Wasn't Abigail going to be mad when she found out that Jenny had really seen God.

The sun was starting to feel hot, but under the big maple tree that shaded one corner of the yard, it was leafy and cool. The tree had a low branch that was just right for sitting. When Jenny was smaller, her father used to lift her up to it. She remembered how scary it had seemed being so high, and yet it had been wonderful at the same time.

"This might be a good place to look for God," said Mr. Bingham. Even though she could climb up by herself now, he swung her up and perched her on the branch.

"I wonder if God climbs trees," Jenny said, delighted with the notion. She looked up, almost expecting to see Him sitting on the branch above hers. No one was there.

"I don't see Him yet," she called down in a disappointed voice. She put her hand up to shade her eyes and glanced all around the yard.

"Keep looking," encouraged Mr. Bingham.

"Not yet," Jenny called down.

"What do you see?" asked Mr. Bingham.

"Lots of green leaves," Jenny reported. She watched a fat caterpillar hunch its way up a twig. "There's a caterpillar up here, too."

"Isn't it amazing that such a furry little fellow will be a beautiful butterfly next spring?" asked her dad.

Jenny agreed that it was amazing, but she still had not found God.

"Look some more," Mr. Bingham urged.

"If I look up, I can see the sky," Jenny told him. Forgetting her search for a minute, she pointed to a fluffy cloud. "Look, that cloud looks just like a unicorn."

In the yard next door, baby Matthew was sleeping in his shaded playpen. Jenny looked down at him and smiled. "Matthew is so sweet. I wish I could hug him. He's so . . . new."

Jenny sighed happily. Even if she didn't see God, it was wonderful sitting in the tree and looking at the world He had made. Suddenly she had an idea.

"I think I get it. Everything is a part of God. God is the tree and the sky and the new baby." She peeked through the leaves at her father, standing below. "And you." She grinned. "And me, too."

Mr. Bingham reached out and lifted her down. "That's what I think, too," he said. "I think your Sunday school teacher meant that you could see God in all the things around you. And I think you are getting pretty big to figure that out."

"I wish I didn't have to get big," Jenny said seriously. "It's scary thinking about it."

"Children have to grow up," said Mr. Bingham. "Every day you will grow and learn new things."

"Mama says the whole family is growing."

"Mama is right," said Mr. Bingham with a nod.

"Will you miss me when I'm grown up and have my own house?" Jenny asked.

Mr. Bingham ruffled her hair. "Wherever you are, we'll come and visit."

"Did you find Him?" Abigail asked with a little smirk when Jenny and Mr. Bingham went back in the house.

Jenny whirled around the kitchen. "He was all over the place," she said, spreading her arms out wide. "After our picnic, I'll show you," she offered, ignoring Abigail's astonished look.

The family piled into the car with the picnic basket and a blanket and headed for City Park. Mr. and Mrs. Bingham settled down contentedly with the Sunday paper at a picnic table. The girls hiked to the pond with a sack of crackers and bread brought from home. Several fat white ducks waddled over, quacking hungrily, as soon as they saw the sack. The wild ducks were slightly less eager, but it only took a few minutes for the cracker sack to empty.

"I wish we could have some ducks," Jenny said wistfully. She hopped backward beside Abigail as they left the pond.

"Ducks are nice," Abigail said. "But Lady would chase them. And they're kind of dirty. We'd have duck doo all over our yard."

"I wouldn't care," Jenny said. "When I get big, I'm going to have a hundred ducks in my yard."

"What are you going to do with all the duck doo?" Abigail giggled.

"I'll make everyone wear boots," Jenny joked.

Halfway to the picnic area the girls stopped. They stretched out on their backs and watched a few fluffy clouds drift across the sky. "I like

Sundays, don't you?" Jenny asked. "I wish every day was like this."

For once, Abigail agreed with her. All their usual disagreements seemed to disappear as they watched the clouds in companionable silence. "I wonder if God is up there, floating around on one of those clouds," Jenny said finally.

"I thought you said He was out in our backyard." Abigail chuckled.

Jenny sat up. "I guess I did think He'd be just walking around wherever I looked. But Daddy showed me all the beautiful things that He made to remind us of Him."

"Like food," Abigail said lightly. "I'm starving."

"I'll race you back to the picnic table," Jenny shouted, already scrambling to her feet so that she had a head start. Panting, the girls reached their parents at almost exactly the same second.

"How did you get so dirty?" Mrs. Bingham exclaimed. She knew her daughter well enough to have come prepared. She took a wet washcloth out of the basket and wiped Jenny's face and hands.

"I was right beside you, and I'm not dirty," Abigail bragged.

"Maybe the dirt jumps on me," Jenny said, squirming to get away from her mother's scrubbing.

"And maybe you jump into the dirt," Mrs. Bingham said with a tolerant smile.

Dirt and ducks were forgotten as the girls sat down to eat. Mrs. Bingham dished up plates of fried chicken, potato salad, and baked beans.

Jenny ate some of her potato salad, trying not to make a face. "Do I have to eat every bite?" she asked.

"Well, maybe not every bite," Mrs. Bingham said. "But most of it."

"How many bites?" asked Jenny, who liked to know exactly what was expected. "How about four?"

Mr. Bingham chuckled. "With the little bites you take, four wouldn't even make a dent."

"How about five bites?" Jenny asked.

"Five big bites," said Mrs. Bingham.

"Why do you let her get away with not eating all her dinner?" Abigail worried about things being fair. "I have to eat all of mine."

"You *want* to eat all your dinner," Mr. Bingham pointed out. He beamed at his family. "This is nice. I'm glad we had a chance to do this before everyone got busy with school."

Jenny took a bite, number four, and looked at Abigail. Her sister was scowling. "I think you're too old to be going to school, Mama," she said. "None of my friends' mothers are going to school."

"Believe it or not, thirty-five is not that old," said Mrs. Bingham with a sigh. "And your friends will get used to it."

Jenny stuffed the fifth bite in her mouth. "Mfft dmm," she shouted.

Mrs. Bingham frowned at her poor manners. Jenny chewed quickly and swallowed. "I'm done," she said again.

"Well, I'm not going to tell anyone," Abigail said crossly. "I think it's silly, going to school when you don't have to."

"Learning is never silly. People should learn new things all their life. It keeps your brain awake," said Mr. Bingham.

Jenny giggled. *"ZZZZ, ZZZZ,"* she said loudly. "My brain is sleeping."

Even Abigail had to smile. Then she started snoring, too. *"ZZZZ, ZZZZ."*

Mr. Bingham offered his arm to his wife. "Well, my dear," he said gallantly, "would you like to take a walk and let these two sleepyheads waste such a lovely day snoring?"

"ZZZZZ, ZZZZZ," the girls snored, even louder. But then Jenny thought of something. "If you go to school, maybe you'll find a best friend. That's what I'm going to do."

"Daddy's my best friend," said Mrs. Bingham.

Mr. Bingham put his arm around his wife and gave her a friendly squeeze. Jenny beamed at her parents. She had the best family in the world. Her life was almost perfect. Only one thing was missing, a best friend of her own. Jenny promised herself that after the first day of school, she would have even that.

— 5 —

The Boss of the World

The night before school started, Jenny was so excited she couldn't eat her dinner. She pushed her French fries around the plate and let out a loud sigh at the meat loaf Mrs. Bingham put on her plate.

Abigail loved meat loaf. She stuffed a large piece of it into her mouth and smirked at Jenny. "Boy, you're a picky eater," she said in her grown-up scolding voice.

"I'm not," Jenny said. "I like pizza and hot dogs and spaghetti."

"You can't have that for dinner every night," said Abigail, who liked almost everything. "It would get boring."

"Not for me," said Jenny. "When I get big, that's all I'm going to ever cook."

"What if your husband wants roast beef and potatoes?" Abigail said.

"Then I'll make him cook his own dinner," Jenny answered.

"Right now, let's eat this dinner," said Mr. Bingham. "You'll be hungry later." The Binghams did not always make Jenny clean her plate, but no dessert or snacks were allowed if she didn't.

"I'm too excited about my best friend," Jenny told her family.

"What best friend?" Mr. Bingham asked.

"The one I'm going to have tomorrow," Jenny said.

Abigail laughed. "You can't get a best friend that easy. Best friends are special. You can't just pick one."

"I'm going to," Jenny said firmly. "That's the only reason I'm going to school."

"Don't you want to learn how to read really well?" asked Mrs. Bingham.

"Well," said Jenny, "maybe. But most of all, I want a best friend. Abigail has two best friends."

"I didn't pick them," Abigail said as she helped herself to more potatoes. "The friendship just grew."

Jenny thought about growing a friend. Planting a tiny little person and watering it like the seeds in the garden. The thought made her giggle.

The next morning Jenny, Abigail, and their mother waited at the end of the driveway for the big yellow bus. "My stomach is full of caterpillars," Jenny said.

"Caterpillars?" Mrs. Bingham looked confused.

"She means butterflies," Abigail explained, sounding superior.

"It should be caterpillars," Jenny insisted. "They're all fuzzy and tickly."

"Would you feel better if I drove you in the car and stayed in your classroom awhile?" asked Mrs. Bingham.

Jenny shook her head. She had been waiting for a long time to ride in the bright yellow bus. Secretly, she was glad that Abigail was with her. Abigail was often bossy with Jenny, and the two girls sometimes argued. But on her first day of school, Jenny was glad to have the company of someone older, who could take charge and show her where to go.

Jenny smoothed the skirt of her new dress and leaned out in the street, looking for the first sign of the bus. She was pleased with the way she looked. Mrs. Bingham had combed her hair shiny and smooth and tied on a bow to match her dress.

Abigail was very fussy about her hair. She liked to curl it with a curling iron. Sometimes she liked to play Beauty Parlor and comb Jenny's hair into fancy styles. But Jenny could never sit still long enough, and the beauty parlor game usually ended in an argument. This morning it had taken Abigail a long time to get ready, and her parents had called her twice to hurry up. Jenny could see she was nervous. She wondered if Abigail's stomach felt funny and squirmy like hers did.

"It's coming, it's coming," Jenny shouted as the bus rounded the curve in the road. Both girls gave Mrs. Bingham a hug, although Abigail looked a little embarrassed. "Have a wonderful day," Mrs. Bingham told them, just as the bus chugged to a stop and the door opened. Jenny liked the wheezy sound it made. She was surprised to see what a big step she had to take to get on the bus. She almost dropped her new purple book bag.

"You should have smaller stairs," Jenny grumbled.

The bus driver smiled. "Maybe you need to grow longer legs."

"Mrs. Dice, this is my little sister, Jenny," Abigail said. "She's starting kindergarten."

Jenny liked the driver's friendly face. It was round and smooth except for a few smile lines around her mouth. She wore her gray hair pulled back in a bun, and there was a smiling face pin on her shirt.

"I'm glad to meet you, Jenny," Mrs. Dice said. "This is bus twenty-three. I'll drive you home after school, too. Your teacher will help you find me after school."

At the next stop, Abigail called to two girls getting on the bus. "Hi, Mandy, hi, Carla." They made their way to the seat in front of Abigail and Jenny. Mandy twisted around in her seat and smiled. "That's a pretty dress," she said to Jenny.

Jenny was so excited she bounced a little in her seat. "My hair bow matches," she said.

"I have a new dress, too," Abigail said.

"It's pretty," Mandy said, scarcely glancing at it. "Are you excited about school?" she asked Jenny.

Abigail frowned as the two fourth-grade girls continued to talk to Jenny. Jenny wondered why her sister looked so unhappy when her friends were being so nice.

As soon as the bus pulled up in front of the school, Abigail grabbed Jenny's hand and marched her to the kindergarten classroom. Jenny hadn't had a chance to say good-bye to Mandy and Carla. "Why are you so mad?" Jenny asked.

"Those are *my* friends," Abby said. "All they did was talk to you. They didn't even notice my new dress. I hope you hurry up and find your own friends."

"I will," Jenny told her. "After today, I'll have my own best friend."

Abby's face softened. "Have fun," she yelled as she ran to catch up with her classmates.

A few children were already in the room. Jenny looked around, not sure what she should do. Then she saw Mrs. Archer. "Good morning, Jenny," the teacher said. "I made you a nice name tag to wear today."

Jenny was insulted. "I know what my name is," she said.

"This is for the other boys and girls. And for me, in case I forget," said Mrs. Archer, pinning it on the front of Jenny's dress. There was a big 23 printed next to her name.

"Oh," said Jenny, embarrassed that she had made such a silly mistake. But Mrs. Archer did not seem upset. "Why don't you look around, or play with the toys until all the other children get here."

A boy with spiky blond hair climbed up on top of a table. "We can't do that in school, Jake," Mrs. Archer said.

"My name isn't Jake," he answered. "It's Superman."

Jenny looked around the room. Kindergarten did seem rather interesting. Several children were looking at a big book of dinosaurs at another table. Mrs. Archer went to the front of the room to talk to a girl who had fluffy hair and was wearing a a pretty pink dress. She was with her mother, and it looked like the girl had been crying.

"I know where the bathrooms are," said a boy with red curly hair and nice brown eyes. "You have to raise your hand if you want to go."

That sounded embarrassing. "I'm not going to raise my hand," Jenny said.

"You have to, or the teacher won't let you go," the boy insisted.

"How do you know?" Jenny asked.

"I know everything about school. I know

where the gym is, too." He looked around the room and finally pointed to a table. "You sit there," he said.

"You're awfully bossy," Jenny said.

"Of course I am. I'm the Boss of the World."

Jenny stared at him in amazement. "Why are you the Boss of the World?" she asked him.

"Because I'm a boy. Boys are always the boss."

"Girls can be the boss, too," Jenny said.

The Boss of the World shook his head. "I'm smarter. I can count to twenty."

"I can count to a hundred." Jenny smiled triumphantly.

"Well, boys are stronger." The boy lifted up the end of a table to prove how strong he was. "See? That's why I'm the boss."

Before Jenny could show him how strong she was, the bell rang. "Find a seat, boys and girls," said Mrs. Archer. "You may sit anywhere you like for now."

Jenny did not want to be near the redheaded boy. She chose a seat by the girl with the pink dress. There was something familiar about her, but Jenny couldn't remember where she had seen her before. Jenny had already decided that she might make a good best friend.

"Hi," Jenny said as she sat down.

The girl put her finger on her lips. "Shhh," she said. "My mother said you're not supposed to talk in school unless you raise your hand."

The girl's eyes were still red from crying. Jenny thought that was an awfully babyish thing to do. She would never cry in school, she told herself. She sat still in her seat and tried to listen to the teacher.

Mrs. Archer told them about some classroom rules. "Every morning, I will call your name to see if you are here," she explained. She showed them an interesting part of the room, filled with blocks and toys. "And these are for everyone to share."

On one side of the room were some little cupboards. "This is where you will keep your coats and hats," Mrs. Archer said. She pointed to signs hanging above each one. "I wrote your names so you would know which one is your special place.

"Now, let's get acquainted," she said. "When I read your name, stand up so we can all see who you are."

Jenny could not remember all the names. But she did learn that the girl with the pink dress was named Elaine. The Boss of the World stood up when Mrs. Archer said "Brian."

"Now, boys and girls," said Mrs. Archer. "We

will take a little walk around the school, so you'll know where everything is."

The teacher lined the class up by twos. Jenny wanted to walk with Elaine. But Mrs. Archer put her beside a girl with a red shirt and long brown braids. Jenny liked the way her freckles marched across her nose, but she couldn't remember her name, and her name tag was too hard to read. Jake was walking with Elaine. He reached in his shirt pocket and pulled something out. "Look what I found," he said.

Elaine squealed so loudly Mrs. Archer hurried back to see what was wrong. "That boy has a bug in his pocket," Elaine cried.

Mrs. Archer soothed Elaine. "Why, it's a cricket," she said. "Jake, maybe you would like to put him in this big bottle, so everyone can see him. He might get squashed in your pocket." The teacher took a bottle with holes in the top from one of the shelves and put the cricket inside.

Jenny was pleased at Mrs. Archer's reaction. Some grown-ups might have made a fuss about pockets full of bugs. But Mrs. Archer had been friendly and not the least bit upset. Jenny noticed that Jake's pants pockets were still alarmingly full. She wished Mrs. Archer would make him show what other treasures he had hidden. But Mrs. Archer was leading them to the girls' bathroom. Right across the hall was the boys'. Jenny wondered why the boys and girls had different bathrooms. At home, Daddy was a boy, and he used the same bathroom as the rest of the family.

"If you have to go, just raise your hand and tell me," said Mrs. Archer.

Jenny looked at the Boss of the World. "I told you," he said out loud.

"Children," Mrs. Archer said sharply. "We never fight at school."

"I wasn't fighting," Jenny said indignantly. "I was showing the Boss of the World how strong I am so I can be boss, too."

Mrs. Archer put her arms around Jenny and the Boss. "I have an idea," she said. "Why don't you be Brian, and you be Jenny, and I'll be the boss."

Jenny nodded in agreement. After a second's thought, Brian agreed also, and the teacher beamed at them. "Now you two can be friends."

Jenny could see by Brian's scowl that he didn't want to be friends. As soon as the teacher turned away, he leaned over and whispered, "I'm still the Boss of the World."

"The teacher said she was the boss," Jenny reminded him.

"She's the boss in school. But I'm the Boss of the World," Brian said. With that, he marched away to play with some other boys.

Elaine was frowning when Jenny sat back in her seat. "I don't like boys," she said.

"Why not?" Jenny asked.

"Boys are noisy and dirty. And dumb," she added.

"Not Brian," said Jenny. "He's smart. And

— 6 —

Jump Rope and Television Stars

Later that morning, Mrs. Archer passed a paper to each student. "After you finish, you may go to the play center," she said. "But be very quiet so you don't disturb the boys and girls who are not finished."

Mrs. Archer explained how to do the paper. "Draw a circle around the thing in each row that is not like the others." Jenny studied her paper. In the first row were a dog, a cat, a lion, and a house. She took her new fat pencil out of her new pencil box. It felt good in her hand. She drew a circle around the house, then peeked at the Boss of the World. He was bent over his paper, humming "Jingle Bells" while he worked.

The next row was harder. On this line there were a knife, a fork, a spoon, and a lion. The knife, fork, and spoon were for eating; Jenny knew that. And lions certainly liked to eat. Jenny thought about the day her parents had taken her to the zoo. The keeper had been throwing big hunks of meat into the cages. The lion hadn't needed any forks and knives. He had used his big, sharp teeth instead. Jenny thought so hard about the lion, she almost forgot her paper. Some of the children had already finished. Jenny quickly drew a circle around the lion.

When she had finally finished all the rows, Jenny looked at the play center. The Boss of the World was stacking blocks with another boy. Jenny had an idea. She would show the Boss of the World how strong she was. Then maybe he would let her be the Boss of the World, too. She walked up behind him and, wrapping her arms around his stomach, she lifted him off his feet.

Brian wiggled and squirmed, but Jenny did not let go. "Hold still," she shouted at him. But his wiggling tipped Jenny over, and down they both fell, with Jenny still holding on.

"Mrs. Archer," called Elaine. "Those kids are acting rowdy."

Jenny didn't know what *rowdy* meant. It sounded like something fun, but Elaine said it like it was something bad.

handsome. I might let him be my boyfriend." She looked at Elaine. "But you could still be my best friend."

"Maybe," said Elaine. "Can you jump rope?"

Jenny nodded. "My sister taught me."

Elaine looked more interested. "I love to jump rope."

At recess Jenny looked for Elaine. She was by the playground fence with a girl named Rachel. They had a long jump rope.

"You and Rachel turn the rope so I can jump," Elaine said. Jenny took the rope and began to turn.

The girl with the red shirt and brown braids stood beside Jenny to watch. Together they chanted as Elaine jumped.

Benjamin Franklin went to France
To teach the ladies how to dance.
First the heel, and then the toe,
Spin around and out you go.

Elaine was a good jumper. Finally she ran out and took the rope so that Jenny could have a turn. "I don't know how to run in," Jenny confessed.

Elaine looked annoyed. But she stopped the

rope until Jenny was in place. Then she and Rachel began to turn, faster and faster. Jenny jumped and jumped, but at last she stumbled when her dress caught in the rope. Tomorrow she would be sure to wear pants, she told herself.

"What's your name?" Elaine asked the girl in the red shirt.

"Crystal Meyers," the girl answered shyly.

"Do you want to jump?" Jenny asked.

"I'm not very good," Crystal answered.

"That's okay," Jenny said cheerfully, in spite of Elaine's frown. "We could turn real slow for you." But before Crystal could answer, Elaine interrupted. "Rachel hasn't had a turn."

Rachel jumped for a long time without missing. Before she ran out of the rope, the bell rang.

"Now it's Crystal's turn," Jenny said.

"We have to go in now," Elaine said, gathering up the rope. "That's what the bell means," she added importantly.

Jenny noticed that all the boys and girls were heading for the school doors. She was embarrassed. "I forgot," she mumbled.

Elaine patted a few loose hairs back in place as they returned to the room.

"You have pretty hair," Jenny told her.

"That's because she's a television star," Rachel said.

Jenny's eyes widened with surprise. "A real television star?"

"You've probably seen me on television," Elaine said. "I'm the Sunshine Shampoo girl."

"We don't watch very much television at our house," Jenny admitted. "But I do like commercials. I thought I'd seen you somewhere before. Sunshine Shampoo really makes your hair pretty."

"I don't even use Sunshine Shampoo. My hair is fluffy because I have a perm," Elaine said.

Jenny stared at Elaine. "But you say in the commercial that you always use it. Why did you fib?"

Elaine looked annoyed. "I'm acting. Someone tells me what to say."

"They shouldn't tell you to fib," Jenny insisted.

Elaine touched Jenny's hair. "Why is your hair so straight?" she snapped. "You should tell your mother to give you a perm like I have."

Jenny had never worried about her hair. It was a soft brown, and even though it was straight, it was shiny and smooth. But so was Abigail's, and she curled her hair every day with the curling iron. Maybe when you had a best friend, you had to be more fussy, especially if your best friend was a television star. "Would you be my best friend if I had curly hair?" she asked.

"Maybe," Elaine said thoughtfully. "I'll have to see it first."

"I like your hair the way it is," Crystal said softly after Elaine had hurried ahead to sit at her table.

Jenny smiled at her. "I like your braids. I used to have braids. But one day I fell asleep with gum in my mouth, and it got stuck in my hair. So my mother had to cut most of it off."

"Elaine shouldn't make you have curly hair if you don't want it," Crystal said. "She's bossier than Brian."

"I want curly hair," Jenny said, even though it was on the tip of her tongue to agree. "Elaine can't help it," Jenny added. "She's just a fussy person."

The morning passed quickly. Jenny was surprised when Mrs. Archer said it was time to go home. "You all did a wonderful job on your papers this morning. You may take them home and show your parents what good work you did today. Tomorrow I would like each student to bring an old shirt for art and a box of tissues to keep in the classroom," Mrs. Archer told them. "I'm giving you a letter telling your parents what I've asked you to bring," she added as she passed two papers to each student.

Jenny was pleased to see a bright gold star at the top of her work sheet. She carefully packed both papers inside her new book bag, feeling very grown-up and proud to be bringing home papers like Abigail. When everyone was ready, Mrs. Archer walked the children across the playground to where the buses were waiting. All the children were still wearing their name tags.

The number of Elaine's tag was 16, but Crystal's had a big *W.* "That means I'm going to walk home," she explained.

Most of the walkers had parents or a babysitter waiting. One girl only had to walk next door. Jenny thought the girl was lucky. It would be nice to live next to the school yard, with all the big swings and teeter-totters. She touched her own name tag, making sure it was still safe. She looked for Abigail. Then she remembered that Abby did not get out of school until three o'clock. At last, she saw Mrs. Dice sitting inside one of the big yellow buses.

Jenny jumped up and waved. "Mrs. Dice," she shouted. "Here I am."

The Boss of the World stood beside Jenny. "That's my grandma," he told Jenny. "I live right next door to her."

Jenny wished her own grandma knew how to drive a big bus. "Hey," she said. "That's how you know so much about school." She climbed up the step to the bus. "I'm going to sit in the first seat."

"I always sit by my grandma," Brian said with a frown.

"Well, there are two seats, silly," Jenny said. "We can both sit here."

Brian plopped himself into the seat next to Jenny, but he didn't look happy.

"Did you like school?" Jenny asked politely as the bus pulled away from the curb.

Brian shrugged. "It was okay."

"Did you get a best friend?" Jenny asked.

Brian nodded. "Jake is my best friend."

"He has a lot of stuff in his pockets," Jenny said.

Brian finally smiled. "He had a candy bar in one pocket, and he gave me half."

"What else did he have in his pockets?" Jenny asked.

"He had some special rocks and rubber bands and a lot of other secret stuff," Brian answered.

"Here is your stop, Jenny," called Mrs. Dice,

before Jenny could learn what sort of secret stuff Jake kept in his pocket. She climbed down the big steps and waved to Brian and Mrs. Dice.

Mr. Bingham was waiting, and he swung her in the air with a big hug. "How was school?" he asked.

Jenny sighed as they walked inside. "I didn't get a best friend yet," she said. "But I might get one tomorrow, if I have curly hair and I'm not rowdy."

— 7 —

Curlers and Kissing Games

The next morning, Jenny hopped in little circles by the front door, waiting for Abigail. Ginger perched on the back of the couch, eyeing her suspiciously.

"Ginger doesn't recognize me," Jenny said.

"That's because you look so glamorous," Mr. Bingham teased. "I hardly recognize you myself." He had helped her comb out her hair because Mrs. Bingham had already left for her first class.

Jenny patted her hair. The curls felt bouncy and smooth against her cheek. She could hardly wait to show Elaine. The night before, her mother had reluctantly curled her hair on big rollers. "Best friends like *you,* not curly hair," Mrs. Bingham had told her.

"But I promised I would," Jenny pleaded.

"Beautiful hair is very important to Elaine. She's the Sunshine Shampoo girl on television." She didn't tell her mother that Elaine didn't use Sunshine Shampoo. Even though Elaine had explained about acting, Jenny wasn't sure her mother would understand.

Mrs. Bingham had still hesitated. "It will be very uncomfortable trying to sleep."

Jenny had continued to beg until her mother gave in. But unfortunately, her mother had been right. Even though the rollers were made out of soft rubber, it had been hard to sleep, and she felt cranky and tired. But she was rather pleased with her looks.

Mrs. Bingham had given her one of her father's old shirts to use as a painting shirt. Jenny checked her bag to make sure she had packed it and the box of tissues. "I'm ready," she announced.

"Abigail, hurry up," shouted Mr. Bingham.

Abigail raced down the stairs and stopped to tie her shoes. "I had to fix my hair," she said, out of breath from running.

"My hair is fixed, too," Jenny said importantly.

Abigail stared at Jenny. "Cute again," she mumbled under her breath.

The girls kissed their father and ran down the

driveway. "I hope you found someone to sit with on the bus," Abigail said crossly. "Because you are not to sit with me. I don't want to listen to all my friends talking about your cute hair."

"I'll sit with Brian," Jenny said. If Abigail was jealous of her hair, Elaine was sure to be pleased.

"Brian?" Abigail teased. "Have you got a boyfriend already?"

Jenny thought about that. "Well, he *is* a boy. And he's a friend. So I guess he's a boyfriend."

Brian was already sitting with another boy, and Jenny had to sit with a bigger girl, who ignored her. As soon as the bus pulled up to the school ground, Jenny waved at Mrs. Dice and ran to find Elaine. She was on the playground with Rachel and another girl, jumping rope.

"I have curly hair," Jenny announced, spinning around to show Elaine.

"Hmmm," Elaine said. "It does look much better. But I've decided to let Rachel be my best friend. Maybe I could let you be my second best friend."

"I don't want to be second best," Jenny said, stamping her foot. Angry tears burned in her eyes.

"Well, gosh. You don't have to get all excited,"

Elaine said. "I can't help it if I already have a best friend."

Just then the bell rang for school to begin. Elaine ran off with Rachel and the other girl, leaving Jenny to walk sadly inside by herself.

"We are going to have fun this morning," said Mrs. Archer. "Today we are going to finger-paint."

Jenny brightened. That did sound like fun. She put on her father's old shirt and watched as Mrs. Archer showed the class how to swirl the paint around into designs.

Elaine was frowning. "I don't want to finger-paint," she said. "I might get it on my clothes."

Jenny was wearing a shirt and shorts today, like most of the other girls. She was surprised that Elaine was wearing another dress.

"Why didn't your mother send a painting shirt?" asked Mrs. Archer. "Did you give her my letter?"

"I forgot it," Elaine admitted. "But I'm very neat. I never get dirty."

Her own mother would be glad to have a girl like Elaine, thought Jenny. Mrs. Bingham often joked that dirt just seemed to leap on Jenny. But Mrs. Archer sounded a little irritated.

"This kind of paint washes off easily," she said. "But we'd better give you something to put over your dress. I don't have an extra shirt, but we can tie this apron around you for protection." She tied an apron under Elaine's arms. It covered everything except her sleeves. Elaine still frowned. She stuck one finger in the paint and made a face.

Jenny felt sorry for her. Mrs. Archer should know that a fussy girl like Elaine wouldn't want to get her hands all dirty.

The thought of getting messy didn't bother Jenny a bit. In fact, she could hardly wait. She imagined that the paint would be squishy and cool, and she wasn't disappointed. She dipped both hands in the paint, enjoying the wonderful feel as she smoothed a big glob on her paper with her fingers.

Brian was drawing a Christmas tree with his fingers. "I like Christmas," he said when he saw Jenny watching him.

Jenny could not decide what to make. Many of her classmates were just swirling the paint around, but Crystal was making a dragon with spikes on his back and a long tail. Jenny drew a flower with a yellow center and lots of red petals. That gave her an idea. If she showed Elaine how pretty her picture was, maybe Elaine would want to try it. She took her paper to Elaine's table and tapped her shoulder. "Look," she started to say. Then she noticed something awful. Where her finger had touched the dress there was a big red spot.

At the same moment Elaine saw the spot, too. "Mrs. Archer," she wailed loudly. "Jenny got me all dirty."

"I'm sorry," Jenny cried. She tried to brush the spot away. But that made the red smear spread.

"Jenny, sit back in your seat," Mrs. Archer said. She took some paper towels and scrubbed at the spot.

Jenny sat down. She felt miserable. She didn't have a best friend, and now her second best friend was angry, and so was the teacher. She swallowed hard to keep from crying.

"The spot is out," Mrs. Archer said briskly. "Elaine, if you really don't want to finger-paint, you may draw a picture with your crayons."

Everyone washed their hands while the paintings dried. Mrs. Archer promised to hang them all up for the whole class to admire. Elaine would not speak to Jenny, even when Mrs. Archer lined all the boys and girls up to go to the playground for recess and Elaine was her partner.

"Are you going to jump rope?" Jenny asked.

Elaine gave her a scornful look. "Not with you. You did that on purpose."

"I did not," Jenny said. She thought Elaine was making an awfully big fuss over a spot that Mrs. Archer had scrubbed away.

"Do you want to play with us?" Crystal asked. Her partner was a girl named Stacy.

"What are you going to play?" Jenny asked.

"Stacy and I are going to chase the boys."

"What do you do if you catch them?" Jenny asked.

"Kiss 'em," Crystal said with a giggle.

"Don't they like to be kissed?" Jenny asked.

"I think they do, but they act like it's awful. After we catch them, then they have to chase us," Crystal answered.

"That's a baby game," Elaine said, walking away with a haughty look.

But it sounded like fun to Jenny. "I'll chase Brian. I'd like to kiss him."

Out on the playground, some of the girls were already running after the boys. "Come here, you little sweetie," Jenny yelled at Brian. "I'm going to kiss you."

"Yuck, Jenny germs," screamed Brian. Obviously, he already knew how to play this game.

Laughing, he raced across the playground, with Jenny in close pursuit. Around and around they ran until the bell rang and everyone crowded back into school, noisy and panting. Elaine gave them all a disapproving look as they filed in.

Jenny folded her hands on her table and tried to sit as still as Elaine. But it was hard. Part of her wanted to sit quietly, but the rest of her wanted to wiggle. At last the bell rang, and it was time to go home.

That night, while dinner was cooking, Abigail practiced her piano lesson. Jenny was stretched out on the living room floor beside Lady. Lady's nose covered part of the book Jenny was reading. "Would you like to hear this story?" asked Jenny. She stroked Lady's head softly while she read. "I wonder if dogs ever feel sad because they can't read," she thought out loud.

Abigail twisted around on the piano bench. "Of course not. They don't even know what reading is."

"Then I'll read to her," Jenny said.

"You're not reading. You've just heard that story so many times you have it memorized."

"I *am* reading," Jenny insisted.

"Girls, please," Mrs. Bingham scolded. She

was sitting at the dining room table studying. "I'm having trouble concentrating. It's been a long time since I've done any homework."

"I liked it better when you didn't do home-work," Jenny said. "There's nothing to do," she said, shutting her book.

Abigail finished her practice. "Come here and I'll show you some notes on the piano."

Jenny jumped up eagerly and sat next to Abi-gail. Her sister pointed to a key in the middle of the piano. "Now this is middle C."

"I want to play a song," Jenny said, running her fingers over some keys.

"You have to learn the notes first," Abigail insisted. "Now start with middle C and go up. The notes are called C-D-E-F-G-A-B-C," she ex-plained as she pushed each key down.

"That's silly," Jenny said. "The alphabet starts with *A*. So why don't you start with middle *A?*"

"You just don't," Abigail answered impa-tiently.

Jenny pushed down some of the lower keys. "I like these notes. It sounds like thunder."

"You have to learn about middle C," Abigail insisted.

"Do you know any thunder songs?" Jenny asked.

"How can I teach you if you won't pay attention?" Abigail shouted.

"You don't have to get so huffy," Jenny said.

"I'm not huffy," Abigail roared.

Mrs. Bingham slammed her book shut.

"Abigail, come and help me with dinner. Jenny, you can set the table."

Meekly both girls followed their mother to the kitchen.

"I know it's hard when things change," Mrs. Bingham said. "But if we all cooperate, it will be much easier."

"I was cooperating," Abigail said. "I was trying to teach Jenny how to play the piano."

"It's too hard," Jenny said. "I had to learn too many new things today. I think my head is stuffed."

"What hard things did you have to learn?" Abigail said scornfully. "Finger-painting?"

"Yes," Jenny exclaimed, delighted that her sister understood.

"That's hard work when you're Jenny's age," Mrs. Bingham said. "Remember, when you were in kindergarten, you were so tired you took a nap when you got home."

Mr. Bingham had been busy all afternoon setting up the new computer for his office. Jenny had already been warned that she must not touch. "It is connected to the computer at the main office through the phone line," Mr. Bingham had explained.

The den had been a good place to play, with an old desk for drawing and some comfortable chairs. It looked very different now. There was a brand-new desk and a copy machine and lots of papers stacked up, waiting to be filed away. It did not seem like part of the house anymore, Jenny thought as she poked her head in the door to call her father to dinner.

The family gathered around the table.

"Finger-painting is baby stuff," Abigail said under her breath to Jenny as she sat down.

"Taking naps is really baby stuff," Jenny said.

"Kissing boys at recess is really, really baby stuff," Abigail said. She turned to her mother. "You should have seen Jenny on the playground today," she said primly. "It's embarrassing. You'd better have a talk with her immediately."

"Hmmm," said Mr. Bingham. "I seem to remember another little girl who liked to kiss. As a matter of fact, the school bus driver complained that it took you so long to get off the bus because you wanted to kiss everyone good-bye."

"I never did that!" Abigail said, her cheeks turning pink.

"I like to kiss boys, Daddy. Especially you and Brian," Jenny said.

"Kisses should be saved for special people," said Mrs. Bingham. "Like your family."

"If two people get married, are they family?" asked Jenny.

Mr. Bingham nodded, and Jenny smiled. "It's all right, then. I think I might ask Brian to get married. He says when he has his own house, he'll have Christmas every day. Of course, we'll have to wait until we're bigger. Maybe when we're twelve."

Ignoring Abigail's snort of laughter, Jenny tried to sneak a green bean off her plate for Lady, who was patiently waiting beside her chair. But just as she slipped it off the table, Abigail noticed.

"She's giving her dinner to Lady," Abigail tattled.

Jenny glared at Abigail. "You're just jealous because no one would even want to kiss you," she said.

"Abigail, don't tattle," said Mrs. Bingham. "And Jenny, eat your dinner. Lady has her own food." She put her fork down and took a sip of coffee.

"Next Tuesday is your first gymnastics lesson," said Mr. Bingham. "Are you excited?"

Jenny bounced up so fast she almost knocked her plate on the floor. She had been so busy with school, she had forgotten about gymnastics. "I'm going to be the best one there," she vowed. "Just you wait and see."

Abigail rolled her eyes. Mr. and Mrs. Bingham smiled across the table at each other. "That's our jumping Jenny," Mr. Bingham said.

— 8 —

Somersaults

At four o'clock the following Tuesday Mr. Bingham drove Jenny to her first gymnastics lesson. Her stomach was doing some weird little flip-flops of excitement. Mr. Bingham had made Abigail come along with them to give their mother a chance to study.

"I don't feel good, Daddy," said Jenny as Mr. Bingham parked the car in front of the youth center.

For once Abigail was understanding. "You're just nervous. I feel sick to my stomach like that when I have to play a piano recital."

Other parents were parking cars, and Jenny saw a girl about ten years old in matching leotards and tights walking into the old brick building. "I don't have a leotard," wailed Jenny. She had thought about what to wear all week and had finally settled on shorts and her T-shirt covered with happy faces. On the front was printed, "Don't worry, be happy." It was her favorite shirt, but right this minute she hated it.

"I'm sure you won't be the only one not wearing a leotard," Mr. Bingham said calmly. "If you really need one we can get it this week."

Abigail looked sympathetic. Jenny knew she understood how important it was to dress like the other girls. "You look all right," Abby murmured encouragingly as they stepped out of the car.

Another girl about Jenny's age walked by with her parents. She looked relieved when she saw Jenny's shorts. She was also dressed in shorts and her shirt had a dinosaur design.

Mr. Bingham led the way into the building, and they followed the crowd of girls to the room where the lessons were held. There was a woman standing by the door holding a clipboard. "I'm Mrs. Landis," she said, peering over the top of dark-rimmed glasses. She checked the clipboard. "You must be Jenny. All the other names are checked off."

Mrs. Landis was not at all the sort of teacher Jenny had expected. She didn't look like the gymnastics stars Jenny had watched on televi-

sion. Mrs. Landis was older than Jenny's mother, and, in spite of her cheerful red leotard and tights, she seemed like the sort of person who would not stand any nonsense in her class. Jenny craned her neck around the teacher to see the other children. Mats were spread on the floor, and people were already somersaulting and turning cartwheels while they waited for the lesson to begin. Jenny had expected everyone to be her age, but there were all different ages, and even a few boys in the class. One of the bigger girls was walking on her hands, and another flipped herself over three times, landing perfectly on her feet every time. Jenny took a deep breath. "I changed my mind. I want to go home. Thank you anyway."

Mr. Bingham's jaw dropped. "But, Jenny, I thought you wanted to take gymnastics lessons."

"Oh, she's just a little nervous," said Mrs. Landis. "That's understandable. She will be fine once we get started." She tried to take Jenny's hand.

Jenny jerked her hand away and ducked behind Mr. Bingham. "I'm not a little nervous," she said. "I'm a lot nervous. And I'm not going in."

"What a baby," Abigail muttered.

Mrs. Landis looked desperate. "Maybe you would just like to watch today."

"No, thank you," Jenny said firmly. "I really want to go home."

Mr. Bingham knelt down beside his daughter. "Mama and I already paid for the lessons," he said. "And it's too late to get our money back. I know it's scary. Anything new is. But if you would just try, you might like it."

Abigail was making soft clucking sounds under her breath. Jenny glared at her. "Stop that this instant, Abigail," Mr. Bingham said.

"If Jenny won't go, can I take the lessons? I mean, since you already paid for them," Abigail asked.

Jenny looked quickly at her father to see his reaction to this request. To her horror, he looked thoughtful. "Well . . . ," he said.

"I changed my mind," Jenny interrupted with all the dignity she could manage. "I'll go in. But just to watch," she warned.

Mrs. Landis smiled. "You can sit on the floor," she said briskly.

Jenny waved good-bye and followed Mrs. Landis. The teacher clapped her hands at the class for attention. "Some of you have taken gymnastics before," she began, "so you know that we always start with some warm-up stretching exercises. All of you new students, don't worry if you can't do everything. Just do the best you can."

"Come and stand by me," said the girl in the dinosaur shirt, with a friendly smile. Jenny liked her shiny black hair and dark brown eyes. But she shook her head and stubbornly stayed where she was.

Jenny watched the class bending and stretching. It did not look very difficult. She was almost ready to join in it after all when Mrs. Landis said, "Everyone line up. We are going to try some forward rolls." Jenny smiled to herself. She had been wise to say she would only watch. She had never even heard of a forward roll.

"Remember to tuck your head," said Mrs. Landis. "And try to land back up on your feet. Like this." The teacher handed her glasses to the girl with the blue leotard and tights Jenny had seen earlier. Then she rolled over in a perfect somersault, bouncing up at the end to stand on her feet.

Jenny watched the line of boys and girls roll down the mat. One boy was almost as good as Mrs. Landis, but Jenny noticed that the girl with the dinosaur shirt had trouble bouncing up. Jenny fought the urge to jump in line. She knew she could do a somersault. She wondered why the teacher called it a forward roll.

Next the class tried cartwheels. Not everyone did as well this time. The girl in the dinosaur shirt especially had trouble. She kept falling sideways. But she didn't give up. Over and over she tried.

Some of the girls laughed at the girl in the dinosaur shirt when Mrs. Landis wasn't looking. But Jenny thought she was very brave to keep trying when she was having so much trouble.

Jenny inched closer to the girl when no one was looking. "Keep your legs straight," she whispered. "Pretend you're a wheel. Like this." Jenny jumped up and did a perfect cartwheel to show her.

"That's wonderful," said Mrs. Landis. Jenny had not even known she was watching. Then, quietly, Mrs. Landis said to Jenny, "You could be a big help to me. Why don't you and Lisa be partners and you can help her with her cartwheels?"

Jenny was amazed. Her first day and already Mrs. Landis needed her help. She glanced quickly at Lisa to see what she thought of the idea. The merry sparkle in Lisa's eyes told Jenny the answer was yes.

"Gymnastics lessons will be a lot more fun with a partner," Lisa said, taking Jenny's hand.

When Mr. Bingham and Abigail picked Jenny up, they were surprised to see her skipping happily out of the gym.

"Guess what?" she shouted. "I was so good I got to be the teacher's helper."

"Oh, brother," groaned Abigail. "Tell me another story."

Just then Mrs. Landis hurried by, carrying a gym bag. "Thank you for helping me today, Jenny," she said. "I hope you'll come back next week and help me again."

Jenny snuck a look at Abigail's startled face. But she didn't say a word. She just skipped the rest of the way to the car with a great big, mysterious smile on her face.

— 9 —

Best Friends and Owl Feathers

One Saturday afternoon at the end of September, Jenny discovered a wiggly tooth. She climbed up on the bathroom counter and sat in front of the mirror to make sure before she told anyone. When she pushed it with her tongue, it hurt a little, but it was definitely loose.

"Abby, come look," she hollered.

Abigail peered into Jenny's mouth. "Yep, it's loose," she said cheerfully. "Want me to pull it out for you?"

Jenny covered her mouth with both hands. "Mmm, mmm," she said, shaking her head.

Abigail shrugged. "Too bad you won't get any money from the tooth fairy."

Jenny uncovered her mouth. "Of course I will. You've gotten lots."

"But you won't," Abigail said wickedly. "The last time the tooth fairy came, I was awake, and I caught her."

"You did?" Jenny gasped. "What did you do with her?"

"I locked her up."

"I don't believe you," Jenny said. "Mama would have found her when she cleaned your room."

Abigail shook her head. "I have a spot so secret that even Mama doesn't know about it."

Jenny ran downstairs to tell her mother. On the way, she tripped over Ginger, who was sound asleep on the bottom stair. Jenny wasn't hurt, but Ginger ran away with a screech. Mr. Bingham was at his office downtown, and Mrs. Bingham had been sitting at the dining room table all afternoon, surrounded by books and papers. "Are you teasing that cat again?" she scolded.

"Make her let the tooth fairy go," demanded Jenny, bursting into tears at the unfairness of it all.

It took a while for Mrs. Bingham to understand the whole story, dry Jenny's tears, scold Abigail, and locate Ginger. But finally calm was restored, and Mrs. Bingham told the girls to play outside. "I have my first test on Monday, and I have to study," she said.

Abigail seemed sorry for teasing. The girls wandered over to the big shade tree in the backyard. "We can play anything you want," Abigail offered generously.

"Let's play house," Jenny decided. "But I get to be the mother this time."

"Wait," Abigail exclaimed. "We're studying about Native Americans in school. Let's pretend that I'm a Sioux princess. We're getting ready for a great feast."

"I want to be a beautiful princess, too," Jenny said. Abigail seemed to have forgotten that this was Jenny's game.

"We can't both be a princess. I know. You could be a pioneer girl. And you're invited to the feast."

"We haven't got food for a feast," Jenny pointed out. "I'll go get some."

"Mama said not to bother her," said Abigail.

"I'll be very quiet," Jenny said as she ran back to the house.

Jenny tiptoed into the kitchen and opened the refrigerator. She found a large bunch of grapes and a jar of pickles that looked interesting. She put them on the kitchen table. Then she pushed a chair to the cupboards. She was reaching for some crackers when her eyes fell on the cookie jar. So she lifted the lid and took a large handful of cookies to finish the feast. She was just climbing down when her mother appeared at the doorway.

"Just what do you think you are doing, young lady?"

Jenny jumped guiltily. "We needed some food for the Sioux to have their feast."

"Put them back," Mrs. Bingham said, pointing to the pickles and cookies. "You may take the grapes. And next time, ask."

"But we didn't want to disturb you," Jenny said.

Mrs. Bingham sighed. "That's very kind of you. But people who don't eat all their dinners do not have cookies in the late afternoon."

Mindful of her mother's watchful frown, Jenny headed back to the trees with the bunch of grapes. She noticed something gray and white half hidden in the grass and stopped to pick it up. It was a feather, the biggest one she had ever seen. "Abby, I found an eagle feather," she cried happily.

Abigail examined Jenny's treasure. "There are

no eagles around here. I'll bet it's from an owl."

Stubbornly Jenny shook her head. "It's an eagle feather."

"Owl."

"Eagle."

"Owl."

Jenny ran back to the house. "Mama, I found an eagle feather," she shouted as she burst through the door.

Mrs. Bingham put her head in her hands. "I thought you were not going to disturb me," she said.

"Oops," said Jenny.

"I think you're big enough to think about other people's wishes," said Mrs. Bingham. "I've asked you to be good while I study."

"I was trying to be good," Jenny wailed. "I just wanted to show you my eagle feather. It's too hard being big all the time."

Mrs. Bingham scooped Jenny up in her arms and gave her a hug. "Sometimes it is hard to be big. But you've been doing a wonderful job."

"I have?" Jenny sniffed.

Mrs. Bingham gave her another squeeze. "You certainly have. And maybe I've been acting too grown-up. What did you say you were playing out there?"

"I'm a pioneer, and Abigail is a Sioux princess." Jenny snuggled into her mother's lap. It felt good to be there. "I found this eagle feather, but Abigail says it's from an owl."

Mrs. Bingham stuck the feather in her hair. They went to the kitchen, and, with a mischievous grin, Mrs. Bingham reached into the cookie jar. "Looks like an eagle feather to me. You'd better get out to the village and tell everyone that big chief Eagle Feather is coming for a visit. And she's bringing a picnic snack."

Mrs. Bingham played with the girls all afternoon. When they went inside, Jenny carefully put away the feather to take to school.

Mrs. Archer's class was having its first Show and Tell that Monday morning. On the bus Jenny showed Brian her loose tooth.

"Gosh, you're lucky. I think you'll be the first one in kindergarten to lose a tooth," Brian said enviously. He tried to wiggle several of his own teeth, but they all remained firmly attached.

"I can push mine out with my tongue." Jenny demonstrated. She pushed with her tongue, and the tooth wobbled and then fell with a plop into her lap.

"Oh, yuck," Brian exclaimed. Jenny grabbed it

and tapped Abigail, who was in the seat directly in front.

Abigail turned around with an irritated look. "Quit pestering," she said fiercely.

"I'm not. I just want to show you my tooth that fell out." Jenny held the tooth for her sister to admire.

"You'd better put it in your pocket," Abigail warned. "If you lose it, you won't get any money from the tooth fairy."

Jenny pocketed the tooth and gave Brian a grin that showed the empty space. "Now I have two things for Show and Tell."

She held up the feather for Brian to admire. Then, without thinking, she reached up and stuck the feather in Abigail's ponytail.

Abigail twisted slightly in her seat and gave Jenny a grouchy look. "I told you to quit pestering," she said. Abigail didn't seem to notice the feather in her hair. Jenny knew her sister wouldn't think it was funny. She decided she had better wait a few minutes before she tried to retrieve it. She sat back in the seat and looked at the things Brian had brought for Show and Tell.

Inside one large bag was something green and prickly. Jenny peeked in the bag and then stared at Brian in surprise.

"That looks like a little Christmas tree," she exclaimed.

"It is." Brian nodded. He opened another sack and dumped it in Jenny's lap. There were the smallest red and green balls Jenny had ever seen, silver and gold bells, and many other miniature decorations.

"They're beautiful," Jenny said, fingering the tiny treasures.

Brian seemed pleased that she liked his collection. "I told you I liked Christmas. I'm going to show everyone how to decorate a tree."

Jenny was still looking at the decorations when the bus arrived at school. She helped Brian stuff them back in the sack. They were the last ones to get off the bus. "Oh, no," Jenny groaned. "I'll bet Abigail will lose my feather."

Jenny worried about the feather all morning. She patted her pocket to make sure the tooth was still safe. Teeth were interesting, but they were tiny, and everyone had teeth. Some people might not be impressed with a tooth. On the other hand, she knew that she was probably the only girl in the class with a real eagle feather. Everyone in the class would be interested in that.

"All right, class," Mrs. Archer said a few minutes after recess. "You may bring your chairs to the sharing circle for Show and Tell."

Mrs. Archer picked Jenny first. There was nothing she could do but show the class her tooth. She demonstrated how she could push the tip of her tongue through the empty space where the tooth had been.

"Gross," Elaine said. "Don't let her pass it around. I don't want to touch her yucky old tooth."

"I think Elaine is right," Mrs. Archer said. "Maybe you could hold the tooth and walk around with it."

Jenny walked around the circle. Most of the children made a face when they saw the tooth. "Are you going to put it under your pillow for the tooth fairy?" Jake asked when it was his turn to look.

Jenny nodded. "My sister got a whole dollar for her last tooth."

"I'll bet the tooth fairy gives me five dollars for my teeth because they're so sharp." Jake wiggled happily in his seat.

"The tooth fairy doesn't ever give five dollars," Elaine said scornfully. "I have something much better than an old tooth to show." Reaching into a sack beside her she pulled out a skirt that looked like it was made from grass. "This is what I wore in the Hawaii Cooler commercial. It's a new soft drink," she explained.

"Do you drink it?" Jenny asked suspiciously.

Elaine gave her a strange look. "Of course. It's delicious."

Jenny watched glumly as Elaine swayed her hips and waved her arms in fancy gestures. Everyone wanted to touch the grass skirt and try doing the hula dance. After that, Jake reached down in his pocket and pulled out a slightly smashed cicada skin.

"My dad says it's like an outside skeleton," he informed the class. "When the cicada grows, the skin splits, and he crawls out with a bigger one. Then he has to sit and wait for it to get dry and hard." He reached in his pockets again, but Mrs. Archer stopped him.

"Let's let someone else have a turn, Jake. You can show us more from your interesting collections next time."

Then Brian showed his Christmas tree. It took a long time because everyone wanted to examine each ornament. But Jenny was sure they would have liked her eagle feather almost as much.

"Does anyone else have anything?" asked Mrs. Archer.

Crystal shyly raised her hand. "I won a ribbon at the state fair this summer," she said. She held up a small clay pig dressed like a farmer, with a straw hat and coveralls. Attached was a beautiful blue ribbon that said "**FIRST PRIZE.**"

"That's amazing," said Mrs. Archer.

Jenny thought the pig was the cutest statue she had ever seen. Its hat was a little lumpy and one leg was fatter than the other. But its face looked just like a pig's with a wrinkled snout. "I love it," she said as Crystal passed it around the circle. "Did you make it all by yourself?"

Crystal nodded. "My mother taught me how, but I did it."

When the recess bell rang, Jenny and Crystal walked to the grassy strip alongside of the playground. "Can you do a backward somersault?" Jenny asked.

Crystal shook her head. "I can do a frontward one," she said.

"I have to practice a backward one for my gymnastics lesson," Jenny explained. "But I can't get my legs over."

"Maybe I could push you over," Crystal offered.

Jenny got into position, and Crystal gave her

a little helping push. But just as they got ready to try again, Elaine came running up.

"Jenny, I've been looking for you," she said. "Would you like to jump rope with us?"

Jenny was surprised at the unexpected invitation, but she nodded happily.

"Can I play, too?" Crystal asked.

Elaine shook her head. "We only want good jumpers."

Jenny did not say anything, even when Crystal gave her an unhappy look. She was afraid that Elaine might not want to play with her either if she insisted that Crystal be included. She tried to tell herself that it was fair, since Crystal didn't know how to jump rope well. But even though she managed to jump "Red Hot Pepper" ten times without missing, it didn't seem like very much fun. Crystal, however, had not stayed unhappy very long. While Jenny was turning the rope for Elaine, she saw Crystal playing tag with Brian and Jake. From the way they were all laughing, Jenny could see that they were having a wonderful time.

—10—

"Little Bear"

After recess the class practiced making *M*'s. Mrs. Archer made the *M* sound. "Can anyone think of a word that starts with mmm?" she asked.

Elaine jumped up without raising her hand. *"Man,"* she said. "M-a-n."

"Very good," said Mrs. Archer. "You even spelled that correctly. But I would have been happier to see you raise your hand."

Jenny squirmed in her seat. She knew how to spell *man,* too. But now the teacher would think she was copying. Then she thought of another word. She raised her hand. *"Me,* m-e," she spelled when Mrs. Archer called on her.

"Very good, Jenny," said Mrs. Archer. "And I liked how you raised your hand."

Mrs. Archer wrote some words on the board. "Can anyone read this sentence?" she asked.

"The man has a red hat," Jenny blurted out.

Elaine glowered at Jenny. "Show-off," she whispered.

Jenny didn't know what to do. Should she pretend that she didn't know how to read the words so Elaine wouldn't think she was showing off? But Mrs. Archer had other ideas. She called Jenny and Elaine up to her desk. "I'm going to work with you both a little. If you are reading as well as I think, I may have you go across the hall and take reading with the first-grade class. Would you like that?"

"My mother already taught me how to read," Elaine said proudly. She seemed happier, now that both of them had been chosen.

Crystal smiled at Jenny when she returned to her seat. "I wish I could read. I love books," she said.

"I'll bet you'll learn how to read pretty soon," Jenny said.

Jenny could hardly wait to tell her mother and father the news when she got home from school. But Mrs. Bingham was at class, and Mr. Bingham had a client in the office. "Change your clothes and play quietly for a while," he said, stepping out of the office. "This is a very important customer. I'll fix us some lunch in a few minutes."

Jenny carefully removed the tooth from her pocket before she put her clothes in the hamper. She put on old jeans and a T-shirt. Then she looked about for something to do. Even though only a few minutes had passed, she was bored and lonesome. Ginger seemed to understand. She rubbed gently against Jenny's leg and meowed a welcome. Jenny sat down and gathered Ginger up in her lap. "You're just like me," Jenny said. "Nobody pays any attention to us."

Jenny showed her tooth to Ginger, but she only sniffed it a little and jumped down off Jenny's lap. Jenny searched in her toy box, but nothing looked inviting. She peeked into Abigail's room as she walked by and saw her sister's horse statue collection displayed on corner shelves.

Jenny went in and picked up one of the small glass statues. "Oh, you're so pretty," she crooned to it. "You look like you should be in a parade." The horse was gold with a silver-white mane and tail. Its front leg was raised, as though it was about to take a prancing step, and its head was set at a proud angle.

Jenny decided to make a parade. She took the horses down and lined them up one by one with the golden one in front. Then she ran to her own room for Mr. Tubbs, her elephant, and her stuffed tiger. She put Mr. Tubbs ahead of the golden horse and the tiger at the very end. Now it would be a circus parade.

"Jenny," Mr. Bingham called from the kitchen. "Time for lunch."

"I'm coming," Jenny yelled. Guiltily she looked at the horses lined up across the room. She knew her father would not think she was very grown-up, getting in other people's things. She knew Abigail would really be angry. Jenny ran out and shut the door. She planned to come back after lunch and put all the horses away.

Abigail was in a terrible mood when she got home from school that afternoon. "Why did you stick that awful feather in my hair?" she screamed as soon as she walked in the door.

"Whew," said Jenny. "I was afraid you'd lose it."

Mr. Bingham came out of his office. "Abigail! Whatever is the trouble?"

"Look what she put in my ponytail this morning," Abigail said, only a little more quietly. She pulled the giant feather from her pocket and showed her father. "She made me look like a geek."

The corners of Mr. Bingham's mouth twitched

a little, but he said sternly to Jenny, "Did you stick this in your sister's hair?"

Jenny nodded meekly. "But it was sort of an accident. I didn't want her to keep it. When I tried to get it back, she was gone."

Abigail made a face. "You did it on purpose to embarrass me."

"I thought it looked pretty," Jenny explained, as her father handed her the feather.

"I have to ask," said Mr. Bingham. "How did you explain the fact that you were wearing an owl feather in your hair?"

Abigail smiled slightly. "I told them it was the latest fad. I said I saw it in a teenage magazine."

Mr. Bingham laughed. "Did they believe you?"

Abigail nodded. "I think so."

Jenny tapped her father's arm. "I think it's an eagle feather."

Mr. Bingham studied the feather. "I'm not really an expert on feathers. Why don't we just say it's from a very large bird."

"Big Bird," Abigail and Jenny said at the same time, remembering their favorite television program when they were younger.

Mr. Bingham went back to his office just as Mrs. Bingham arrived home, loaded with grocery sacks. She had gone shopping after class.

"Did you take your test?" both girls asked together as they helped put the food in the cupboard.

Mrs. Bingham looked so sad that for a minute Jenny felt a pang of guilt. What if her mother did badly on the test because she had played with them instead of studying? But then Mrs. Bingham reached into her notebook and pulled out a paper. "Tah dah!" she said gaily.

The girls exclaimed over their mother's excellent test score.

A large A was scrawled across one corner. "Are you going to pin it on the refrigerator?" Jenny asked. The Binghams' refrigerator served as a family bulletin board and art gallery.

"Why not?" asked Mrs. Bingham proudly. "I deserve it." After the paper was held in place with a magnet, Mrs. Bingham and Abigail went to change their clothes. Suddenly Abigail screamed. At that very minute, Jenny remembered the horses. She had forgotten to put them away. She ran up to her sister's room.

"Look what you did to my room," Abigail fumed.

Jenny hung her head. "I'm sorry. Really I am. I'll put them all back." She reached for a statue

PTO
News

to replace it on the shelf, but she was so anxious, she tripped over Mr. Tubbs the elephant, still in place at the head of the parade. She didn't fall, but her foot stumbled into the golden horse. Sadly she picked it up. "Its leg is broken," she sobbed. "I didn't mean to break it."

Now both girls were sobbing. Mrs. Bingham picked up the pieces of the statue. "I think we can fix it," she comforted Abigail.

Jenny was sent to her room in disgrace. But even that punishment could not make her feel worse than she already did. When she was allowed downstairs, she still felt awful. Abigail would hardly speak to her.

Jenny perched sadly on the kitchen stool while her mother prepared dinner. "Tell me about school today," said Mrs. Bingham.

Jenny was surprised her mother would even want to talk to her. She poked her tongue through the empty place in her mouth, and for the first time her mother noticed the missing tooth.

"I'll show you my tooth," Jenny exclaimed after her mother had admired the empty space. She ran upstairs and stopped at her bedroom door, trying to remember where she had left it.

"It's gone," Jenny wailed. "I lost my tooth, and

now the tooth fairy won't leave me any money."

"Serves you right for breaking my horse statue," Abigail hissed. Nevertheless, she helped Jenny search her room to see if the missing tooth had fallen on the floor.

"Maybe you could draw a picture of it and leave it under your pillow," suggested Mrs. Bingham.

"Would the tooth fairy like that?" Jenny said, brightening a little.

"I'll bet she would," Mrs. Bingham said. "After dinner you can draw it for her."

"I might get to go to the first grade for reading," Jenny said, once they were back in the kitchen. "I could read you a story right now."

"That sounds lovely," said Mrs. Bingham. Jenny found one of her favorite books and returned to the kitchen. Her mother and Abigail were peeling vegetables at the sink. Jenny started reading the book to her mother.

"I told you before, that's not really reading," said Abigail. "You've just heard it so many times you know all the words." She went to her room and came back with a book. "This is one of my old ones," she said with a smirk. "Let's see you read this."

Jenny looked at the cover. *"A Kiss for Little Bear,"* she read slowly. Abigail stared in surprise.

Jenny began reading. She read slowly, and she needed help with a few of the words. But she finished the whole book. After the first few pages, Mrs. Bingham stopped fixing the vegetables and stood by Jenny's chair to listen. "That's wonderful," she said. "I didn't know you could read that well."

"Neither did I," said Jenny.

Mr. Bingham came to the kitchen to help cook dinner. Jenny read the book again.

"Amazing," said Mr. Bingham. "That's the best story I ever heard."

Jenny read *A Kiss for Little Bear* to her family two more times before she went to bed. But, just as she climbed under the covers, she remembered that she hadn't drawn her tooth.

"You don't need to, anyway," Abigail said, coming into her room. She handed her the tiny white tooth. "You left it in my room when you got into my horses," she said grimly.

Jenny slipped it carefully under her pillow. "I'm sorry I did that. But I didn't have anything to do. I hate it when Mama's gone at school."

Abigail sat down on the edge of Jenny's bed.

"It's just because we're not used to it," she said. "I thought it was kind of dumb at first. But it's nice having Daddy home so much."

Jenny snuggled sleepily into her covers. "I still think it was nicer when I was little and I didn't have so many troubles."

Abigail laughed. "What kind of troubles could a kindergarten baby have?"

Jenny sat straight up and glared at her sister. "I am not a baby. And I do so have worries. What if I never get a best friend? What if I never learn how to do a backward roll? And what if Mama is so busy with school that she forgets my birthday?" Jenny's birthday was coming up in October. She plopped back down, her head suddenly heavy with all those worries.

Abigail gave her a friendly punch. "You are such a silly," she said affectionately. "You'll get a best friend. And if you practice hard, you'll probably be able to do a backward roll. And Mama would never forget your birthday, no matter how busy she is."

"Are you sure?" Jenny mumbled sleepily.

"Positive," Abigail said firmly. "Now go to sleep."

Jenny burrowed into her covers. But then she

popped back up. "What if the tooth fairy forgets my tooth?"

Abigail giggled. "Then I really will catch her and lock her up."

But Abigail did not have to capture the tooth fairy after all, for the next morning, when Jenny reached under her pillow, the tooth was gone, and there was a crisp dollar bill in its place. She raced downstairs and almost crashed into Mr. Bingham as he walked to the breakfast table.

"Whoa," he laughed. "What's all this excitement?"

"The tooth fairy left me a whole dollar. Just like she did for Abigail, Daddy," Jenny exclaimed, proudly showing him the crisp one-dollar bill.

"Gosh," Mr. Bingham said. "When I was a boy, she only brought me a quarter."

Jenny stopped and stared at him. "Did your tooth have a cavity?"

Mrs. Bingham laughed. "Put the dollar in your piggy bank so it doesn't get lost, and you can think about what you would like to spend it on."

Jenny told Brian about the dollar on the bus ride to school. "A whole dollar?" he repeated wistfully. He wiggled his teeth to see if any had gotten loose since the day before.

"I'll bet they fall out pretty soon," Jenny said comfortingly. "I'll read you a story so you don't have to think about it." She read *A Kiss for Little Bear* to Brian all the way to school. Then she read it to Crystal at recess. Both of them agreed it was the best story they had ever heard.

After recess Mrs. Archer had a surprise. "Today is Paul's birthday, and to help him celebrate, his mother is bringing a special treat," she said. Mrs. Archer put a paper crown on Paul's head, and the whole class sang "Happy Birthday."

Paul wiggled with embarrassment, but Jenny thought he looked terribly pleased just the same. Then Paul's mother arrived with a huge box of cupcakes. Paul passed them out to the class while his mother and Mrs. Archer poured cups of fruit punch.

"I had a surprise party," Paul told the class. "All my cousins came and my friends from next door. They all hid, and then they jumped out and yelled 'Surprise!' "

"My birthday is October twentieth," Jenny said out loud. "Maybe I'll get a surprise party."

"It won't be a surprise if you already know," Crystal said.

Jenny thought about that while she ate her cupcake. Abigail was sure their parents would never forget her birthday. But her mother was very busy now that she was going to school, and her father was busy with his new office arrangements. Jenny was still a little worried. Maybe she should remind them. But if they were planning a surprise party, it would spoil everything if she knew.

After everyone was finished with their cupcakes, Mrs. Archer announced she was going to read them a story. Jenny wiggled in her seat. Sometimes she forgot to raise her hand when she wanted to talk, but this time she remembered. She waved it back and forth, and at last Mrs. Archer noticed.

"Could I read the class a story?" Jenny asked. She showed Mrs. Archer the book.

Mrs. Archer looked doubtful, but when Jenny read the first page, she nodded. The class took their chairs to the story corner and made a circle around Jenny. Jenny read the words, stopping at each page to show them the pictures.

"That was wonderful," exclaimed Mrs. Archer when Jenny had finished.

Jenny could tell that everyone liked the story, even Elaine. The next day she brought the book back to school and took it outside at recess in case some of her classmates wanted to hear it again.

On their way outdoors, they passed several bigger girls with feathers stuck in their ponytails. "Why have you got feathers in your hair?" asked Jake.

The big girls patted their hair. "It's the latest style," they explained.

Jenny had to squeeze her lips shut to keep from laughing. "Come on," she said to Crystal.

Just then Abigail came out of the girls' rest room. "Thank heavens I found you," she whispered. "Where's the feather?"

"What do you care?" Jenny asked. "You said it was dumb and ugly."

"I changed my mind. Everyone thinks it's a great style. I need it. Besides, it's your fault I got into this mess."

Jenny reached in her pocket. She had brought the feather for the next Show and Tell. But she remembered the broken horse statue, and she knew Abigail was right about the feather. Silently she handed it to her sister.

"Gee, thanks," Abigail said. She looked surprised that Jenny had given it to her so easily.

"That's okay," Jenny said. Even though it seemed she would never be able to use the feather for Show and Tell, somehow she felt better inside. And Abigail, instead of looking at her like she was a pest, was smiling like a friend.

"See you at home," Abigail said as she stuck the feather through her ponytail.

Crystal walked with Jenny to the shady trees that bordered one side of the playground. Jenny sat down. "Are you ready to hear the story again?" she asked Crystal.

Crystal looked at the boys and girls running around the playground. "Wouldn't you rather chase the boys?" she asked longingly.

"Don't you like listening to my story?" Jenny asked.

"Oh, yes," Crystal said quickly. "But you've read it a lot of times."

Crystal looked unhappily at Jenny, as if she were worried that she had hurt Jenny's feelings. But instead, Jenny closed the book with a smile and a large sigh of relief.

"Hooray," she said. "I was getting awfully tired of reading it. Let's go get those boys."

—11—

Jenny's Bad Word

After a whole month of class, most of the kindergarteners felt that they knew everything about school. They could take a note to the office for Mrs. Archer without getting lost. Most of the time, they remembered to raise their hands when they wanted to talk. They even knew what to do in case of fire because there had already been two fire drills.

But one day Mrs. Archer had a surprise. "How many people are afraid of storms?" she asked.

Most of the class raised their hands. "My aunt's roof blew off in a tornado," a girl named Jessica told the class.

"My dog hides under the bed," Brian offered. Then he added, "Sometimes I hide with him."

"I don't like thunder," Jenny admitted.

"Most storms are not dangerous if you know

what to do," said Mrs. Archer. "Captain Carson of the New Albany police force is coming to school today to talk about how to behave in a storm."

Everyone agreed that this would be a good idea.

Mrs. Archer read them a funny story. Jenny noticed that Elaine wasn't sitting quietly as usual. She squirmed in her chair and looked miserable and cranky.

"We have another birthday," said Mrs. Archer when the story was done.

This time it was David. Mrs. Archer let him wear the birthday crown, and the whole class sang "Happy Birthday." David's mother brought cookies for the class, special bakery cookies with candy faces. Jenny bit into hers, wishing each child could have two. They were chocolately-melt-in-your-mouth good. But when David handed one to Elaine, she pushed it away. "I don't like this kind of cookies," she said crossly.

Jenny was shocked. Elaine was always so mannerly.

Mrs. Archer looked surprised, too. "Just say 'No, thank you' if you don't want any," she said.

After the treat, Mrs. Archer handed out papers with big, fat elephants on them to color and cut out. Jenny looked through her crayons for an interesting shade. Finally she selected a purple crayon, and, after some more thought, took a pink one for the elephant's ears.

"Elephants are gray," Elaine said scornfully. "Don't you know that?"

"Gray elephants are boring," Jenny said mildly, starting to color with the purple crayon.

"I'm making mine with polka dots," Jake added.

"Mine is orange." Crystal held her paper up for everyone to see.

"Well, you are all so dumb," Elaine grumbled loudly. She pushed so hard on her gray crayon that the tip broke off with a snap. Suddenly Elaine burst into tears.

Mrs. Archer came over and put her hand on Elaine's forehead. "Are you feeling sick?" she asked.

"Yes," said Elaine, crying even louder. "I've been sick all morning. My head hurts, and I think there are fleas in this stupid school."

"Fleas?" Mrs. Archer looked surprised.

"They're biting me," wailed Elaine. "I itch all over."

Just talking about fleas made Jenny's arm start

to itch. She scratched, but stopped when she saw Elaine glaring suspiciously at her. She didn't want Elaine to say the fleas came from her.

Mrs. Archer looked at a small pink spot on Elaine's arm. "I think you might have chicken pox," she said kindly. "It's nothing to worry about, but let's go see the nurse and call your parents."

"I don't think my mother will allow me to have chicken pox," Elaine wailed.

Mrs. Archer patted Elaine's back. "Just about everyone gets chicken pox," she said. "It will be all right." At the door she paused and looked back at the class. "The rest of you boys and girls stay very quiet and finish making your pictures. I'll be right back."

For a minute the room was silent. Then Jake stood up and crowed like a chicken. "I am the monster chicken pox," he announced, crowing again.

Some people laughed, but most of them went on working. Everyone knew that Jake had trouble sitting still. Mrs. Archer had to scold Jake more than anyone in the room.

Jenny colored her elephant's ears. Then she heard a noise from the other side of the room and looked up. Jake was still pretending to be a chicken pox. But now he was walking around the room pinching people, pretending to bite. When he got to Brian, he pinched him on the arm. But Brian stood up and pushed Jake away. Jake fell backward and sat down hard on the floor between the desks. Jake said a bad word, very loudly, just as Mrs. Archer came in the room.

Jenny watched to see if Mrs. Archer had heard the bad word and what she would do.

"I'm very disappointed in you," said Mrs. Archer. "Return to your seat at once."

"But Brian pushed me," Jake protested.

"I said go to your seat, I'll talk to you later." The teacher's voice was usually soft and sweet, but not now. Jake meekly went back to his seat.

"Elaine's mother is going to take her home until she is feeling better," Mrs. Archer told the class. "I would like everyone to put down your crayons for a while. My friend Captain Carson is here to talk to you. Afterward we will have a tornado drill. Now remember, it is just for practice, like we did with the fire drill."

A tall policeman came to the door, and Mrs. Archer motioned for him to come in.

Captain Carson noticed some worried faces. "You have probably heard about tornadoes on the news. It's not storming today, but it's always good to know what to do."

First Captain Carson talked about thunder and lightning.

"Most children are afraid of the thunder. Thunder can't hurt you. It is only the noise of the lightning. Sometimes people try to hide under trees," he went on. "But lightning hits the highest point around. So you must never hide under a tree. Try to get inside. Does anyone know what to do if you are outside and can't get in?"

Jenny had seen that on the news one day. "You try to find a ditch or a hole, and you cover your head," she said when Captain Carson called on her.

"Very good," he said.

Jake raised his hand. "I'm going to be a policeman when I grow up," he said.

Jenny forgot to raise her hand. "You'll have to stop biting people and saying bad words," she said. She tried to think about a grown-up Jake in a policeman's uniform. Maybe he could give all the bad guys chicken pox.

Captain Carson talked about tornadoes. "Luckily, Ohio does not have a lot of tornadoes. But we do have some." He told them to go to their basements if they were at home during a tornado. "If you haven't got a basement, go to an inside hallway," he said. "It's important to stay away from windows in case they break. That's what we will do in school, too," he said. "Then you will crouch down and cover your heads." Mrs. Archer got down on her knees and covered her head to demonstrate. Jenny almost giggled to see her teacher like that. She listened for the siren. The class had already had a fire drill. On that day, they had filed out the door quietly and gone to the playground. This sounded like a lot more fun.

Even though the class was waiting for the siren, when it came, everyone jumped. Mrs. Archer hustled them into the hallway, and the whole class crouched down beside the walls.

"This is fun," Jenny whispered to Crystal.

"I think it's scary," Crystal said.

Since Crystal had admitted feeling frightened, Jenny didn't feel like such a baby to say that she was a little scared, too.

"What about Elaine?" Jenny said. "She won't know what to do if there's a tornado."

"She wouldn't like to get on the floor anyway," Crystal said. "She'd worry about getting dirty."

"I'd protect her," said Jake. "I'd push her down."

On the way to her gymnastics lesson that afternoon, Jenny had lots of news to tell her mother. She was trying to tie her shoe as she talked. She could tie a bow pretty well, but some days she had trouble. This was one of those days. Every time she pulled one side of the bow, the other side slipped out. Each time it happened, Abigail snickered. After the third time, Jenny was so angry she said Jake's bad word.

There was a minute of shocked silence. "People who say words like that are too dumb to think of a better word," said Mrs. Bingham calmly. "I'll bet you're smart enough to think of a better word than that."

"Like what?" Jenny asked.

"Oh, you have to think of it yourself, or it isn't any good. Something that sounds awful."

"How about *scrunch?*" said Abigail.

"I've got a better one," Jenny shouted. *"Pickle."*

"That sounds good," Mrs. Bingham said as they pulled up in front of the gym. "So from now on, that can be your mad word."

"Mama, my bow came out again," said Jenny. "Pickle, *pickle,* PICKLE."

—12—

McFreckle's

That Friday night, Mr. and Mrs. Bingham announced that they were going out. "It's our anniversary," Mrs. Bingham explained. "Daddy is taking me to a romantic dinner."

"Who's going to baby-sit?" asked Jenny. The Binghams did not go out very often, and Jenny didn't like being left with baby-sitters. On that one thing she and Abigail were agreed, although in Abigail's case, it had more to do with thinking she was too old.

"I asked Melissa," said Mrs. Bingham, naming a high school girl who lived on the next block.

This news cheered Jenny. She liked Melissa, a friendly redhead who played games and read to them, unlike other baby-sitters, who talked to their friends all night on the phone. Still, Jenny did not like for her parents to leave. "Why can't we go with you?" she said. "We'd like a romantic dinner, too."

"It wouldn't be romantic with you along," Abigail snorted.

Jenny put her hands on her hips. "It would so," she shouted. To her mother she said, "I wouldn't mind if you did a lot of kissing and stuff."

Her mother took a silky red dress out of the closet. "You two scoot downstairs and watch for Melissa while Daddy and I get dressed." She gave Jenny a quick squeeze. "You'll have a lot more fun with Missy than watching us."

Jenny suspected that her mother was right. Still, she stomped just a little as she walked downstairs, to let her mother know she was not happy about her leaving.

Missy knocked on the door, and Jenny answered. A hot gust of humid wind swirled into the house when she opened the door. Shutting it behind her, Missy shook a few drops of rain from her hair like a dog. "It sure is hot for this time of year," she said. "But maybe the rain will cool it off."

"Let's go downstairs." Jenny tugged, pulling Missy toward the basement door.

"Why do you want to play in the basement?" Missy asked.

"Dad put some mats down for Jenny to practice her gymnastics," Abby explained.

"I have to learn how to do a backward roll before my next lesson," Jenny said. "I'm just about the only one who can't do it now."

"Maybe I could give you some tips," Missy agreed. "I used to take gymnastics lessons."

By the time Mr. and Mrs. Bingham were dressed in their evening finery and ready to leave for the restaurant, Jenny had almost mastered the backward roll.

"Look at me," she exclaimed when her parents came down to say good-bye. Placing her hands beside her head, she flipped herself over. The landing was slightly wobbly, but there was no doubt she had finally learned.

"That's my girl," said Mr. Bingham. "Instead of Jumping Jenny, maybe we should call you Rolling Jenny."

"Backward Rolling Jenny," Abigail teased.

"I'm proud of you," said Mrs. Bingham. "You worked at it and didn't give up." She kissed her daughters good-bye. "Have fun with Missy. We won't be late."

Jenny gave her parents a hug. She loved the silky rustle of Mrs. Bingham's fancy dress and the smell of her perfume. And her father looked handsome in his crisp gray suit.

Missy stayed in the basement with the girls, teaching them other gymnastics tricks. Suddenly she looked at the small, ground-level windows. "Wow. It must be later than I thought. Look how dark it is. I'd better fix our dinner."

"I wish I could cook dinner," said Jenny.

"Well," Missy said doubtfully, "maybe you could help."

Jenny knew just what she wanted. "Let's fix macaroni. The box kind," she said as they walked upstairs.

"It's not late," called Abigail, who was the first to reach the kitchen. "It's just this dark because there's a storm coming."

Unhappily, all three girls looked out the window. Ohio often had sudden thunderstorms, but this one looked especially threatening. Under a rolling, dark sky, the world looked purple and wild. Already a few small branches had broken off the trees and were tumbling in the wind.

"I don't like storms," Jenny said as the first thunder rumbled in the distance.

Lady didn't like storms either. As the next thunderclap rumbled, she tucked her tail under her and ran to Jenny's room to hide under the bed. Ginger, however, slept cozily in a chair, trusting her humans to protect her from any harm.

Somehow the peacefully sleeping cat cheered the worried girls. "Let's get dinner going," Missy said briskly. "That will keep our minds off the storm." She bustled about the kitchen, putting the water on to boil for macaroni.

Abigail sliced some tomatoes and set the table while Jenny watched the water, waiting to pour in the macaroni. Everyone tried not to think about the storm, growing steadily worse as they worked. But it was hard to ignore the darkness and the howling wind. Jenny poured in the macaroni, and Missy helped her stir.

"Captain Carson told us what to do in case of tornadoes," Jenny remarked. "If we hear the siren, we should go downstairs."

"I think it's just a thunderstorm," Missy said nervously. "But maybe we should listen to the weather report." She reached to turn on the radio.

Crack! There was a burst of lightning and thunder so close it rattled the windows. All three girls gave a squeal of fright, and another, as the lights went out, plunging the house into gloom.

Missy was the first to recover. "Stay calm. We'll probably have the electricity back in just a minute," she said, trying to sound cheerful. She switched on the big emergency flashlight the Binghams kept plugged into the wall, and a ghostly light filled the room. Then she carefully switched off the burners on the stove. The girls sat close to each other, jumping at every thunder crack.

"Try to think about something else," Missy said. She was so white, her freckles stood out like polka dots on a ghost.

"I like your freckles," Jenny said. "I wish I had some."

The color returned to Missy's face. "I can arrange that," she said cheerfully.

She took a washable marker from one of the kitchen drawers and drew tiny freckles on Jenny's face. "Draw some on me, too," Abigail said.

While Missy was busily drawing the freckles, the storm slowly passed. But, although the thunder and lightning was moving farther away, the electricity was not restored.

"The stove went out before the macaroni got done," Missy drained the macaroni and tasted a bite. "It's a little chewy, but we can eat it." She

helped Jenny pour in the cheese mix, milk, and butter. "I think it's warm enough to melt the butter," she said. "You can stir it while I get some bread."

Jenny remembered that Mrs. Bingham always added a little pepper. She picked up the shaker and shook it into the macaroni. But it was too dark by the stove to see how much was going in. Jenny shook and shook until Missy noticed and yelled, "That's enough." Then Jenny looked in the pan.

"Ohh, ohh," she said. "I think maybe I did put a tiny bit too much in here."

"Tiny bit!" Abigail exclaimed. "It's freckled, just like our faces."

The girls stared at the ruined dinner. "We'll have to try it," Missy said. "We can't cook anything else. Maybe Jenny has invented a new dish. Freckled Macaroni."

Seeing Jenny's forlorn face, Abigail tried to cheer her up, too. "You could open a restaurant. Maybe we'll all get rich."

Jenny began to smile. "We could call it McFreckle's."

Missy dished up the dinner, and the joking faded. "Well, who's going to taste it?" she asked.

"Not me," Jenny said firmly.

"I guess I will," Missy said bravely. But before she could force down the first bite, the door opened and two dripping wet parents burst in.

"We were worried," explained Mr. Bingham.

"Some trees were knocked down, and electricity was out all over town. When we tried to call, the phone was knocked out, too," Mrs. Bingham continued. "We thought you would be scared to death."

"We weren't scared a bit," Jenny boasted. Then, seeing the look on Abigail's face, she added, "Well, not very much."

Mr. Bingham looked into the pan. "What's for dinner? I'm hungry."

"I don't think you'd better eat that, Daddy," said Abigail. She rolled her eyes at Jenny. "She made it."

The kitchen light blinked once and then came on, flooding the room with welcome brightness. Mr. Bingham took a closer look at the freckled macaroni.

"This really looks delicious," said Mr. Bingham bravely. "But I did promise your mother a dinner out. Maybe we should all go out together."

"What about your romantic dinner?" asked Jenny.

"I think we can put off the romance until a

sunshiny day." Mrs. Bingham laughed, as she dried her hair with a paper towel. "I'm not sure that I look properly romantic with water dripping off my nose."

Jenny leaned over and whispered something to her father. "Of course Missy is coming," said Mr. Bingham. "I do have one request, however."

They all waited.

"I think everyone except Missy should wash off their freckles."

"Oh, my gosh," said Abigail, putting her hands on her face. "What if someone had seen me like this?"

"It would have been all right," Jenny said seriously. "You could just tell them that you read in a teen magazine that freckles were the latest style."

—13—

A Secret and Some Fun

"Crystal's mother called while you were at your gymnastics lesson," Mrs. Bingham said Tuesday night after dinner. "Would you like to play at her house tomorrow afternoon?"

Jenny nodded happily. It was the first time she had been allowed to go to someone's house all by herself. "I'm glad Crystal and I don't have the chicken pox. A lot of the kids are getting it. We're going to jump rope. Crystal wants to practice so Elaine will let her jump with us."

"My little Jumping Jenny is the right person to do that." Mr. Bingham chuckled.

Jenny jumped over to her father and gave him a hug. Mr. Bingham picked her up and swung her around in a circle. "Pretty soon you'll be too big for me to lift," he said, panting a little.

"I need to talk to you," Abigail said to Mrs. Bingham. "It's important."

"We can talk while we do the dishes," said Mrs. Bingham.

That sounded interesting. Jenny trailed after them to the sink. But Abigail stopped her. "This is private," she said. "Don't be such a snoop."

Jenny was indignant. How could Abigail say such a thing? She had never snooped.

"Why don't you take Lady outside?" Mr. Bingham suggested. "I have to do a little paperwork in my office."

Jenny reluctantly called Lady. Then she went to the closet to get a jacket. She took a lot of time putting it on so she could listen, but her mother was running water in the sink, and it was hard to make out the words. Jenny thought she heard the word *present,* and then the word *surprise.* Suddenly she understood. Abigail was going to give her a real surprise party, and she was asking their mother to help.

Jenny went out the front door so Abigail wouldn't know she had been listening. She raced from one end of her yard to the other, whirling around every few feet in a joyful dance. Lady was not sure what all this running was about, but she raced along beside her, barking with excitement.

Finally Jenny flopped on the ground. She felt the scratchy grass beneath her, dry now with the coming of autumn. A few leaves on the maple trees were streaked with red and gold, waiting for the first frost to send them tumbling down. Jenny patted Lady, sitting patiently beside her. "I am happy, happy, happy," she said. Lady's brown eyes seemed to understand that sometimes growing up seemed pretty scary. But right now it was the most wonderful thing in the world.

Abigail stepped outside. "What are you doing?" she asked. "I saw you running around like a wild person."

"I was doing a happy dance," Jenny answered.

"Well, stop it," said Abigail. "If anyone saw you, they would think you were some kind of weirdo, leaping all over the yard like that."

"I *have* stopped," Jenny pointed out. It was on the tip of her tongue to say something mean, but she closed her mouth just in time. Then she sighed. It was two more weeks until her birthday. How would she stand being nice to Abigail until then?

Fortunately for Jenny, she had the visit to Crystal's house to occupy her mind. The next day she could hardly sit still, and she was so noisy during story time, Mrs. Archer had to scold her twice.

"I'll show you my baby hamsters," Crystal promised at recess. "And my mom's going to make us some popcorn for a snack."

After school Jenny showed Mrs. Dice the note her mother had written. "I'm not going on the bus today," Jenny said proudly. "I'm going to walk home with Crystal."

"Have fun," Mrs. Dice said as she closed the bus door.

Brian waved out the bus window. "See you tomorrow," he yelled.

Crystal's house was only four houses away from the school. "Let's hop all the way," suggested Jenny.

"Let's jump backward," Crystal challenged her. "I'll bet I can do it faster than you can."

"No fair peeking," Jenny shouted gleefully, making one last check to see that the sidewalk was clear. Away they went until they reached Crystal's door, panting and tired, at exactly the same time.

"My goodness," said Crystal's mother, opening the door for them. "Why are you both so worn out?"

"We had a backward jumping race," Crystal explained between gasps for breath.

"That sounds like fun," Crystal's mother said. "Who won?"

"We both did," the girls chorused.

"You must need some re-energizing," Mrs. Meyers said. She led them to a clean but cluttered kitchen and, after pushing aside a pile of interesting-looking paints, clay pots, and tools, gave them each a tall glass of milk and a bowl of chicken soup. For dessert there were chocolate chip cookies.

"My mother is an artist," Crystal explained when she saw Jenny looking around the messy kitchen.

"What kind of pictures do you paint?" Jenny asked politely.

"Not all artists paint," Mrs. Meyers explained. "I make things out of clay or wood. Sometimes I even work with cloth."

"I want to be an artist when I grow up," Jenny said. "The regular kind that makes pictures."

"Jenny draws great pictures," Crystal said.

Jenny smiled at her, pleased that she'd noticed. "So do you."

"Crystal wants to be an artist, too," Mrs. Meyers said, showing Jenny several small clay animals her daughter had made. Jenny picked up a tiny mouse with a sharp little nose and big, round ears. "It's so pretty," she crooned. "I wish I could do that."

"Maybe we can play with some clay later," Crystal said. Then she grabbed Jenny's hand. "But first come and see my baby hamsters." She took Jenny to her room. Inside a small cage on the dresser was a small brown hamster mother, curled up around four tiny babies.

"Would you like one?" Crystal asked.

"I wish I could," said Jenny wistfully. "But Daddy says he has enough mouths to feed already."

When Crystal and Jenny went back to the kitchen, they discovered that Mrs. Meyers had spread some papers on a table for them. She gave them some cool, slippery clay. Crystal showed Jenny how to roll the clay between her hands to make a snake. Soon the table was covered with snakes and an assortment of strange, lumpy creatures. Then they made snake bracelets and pretended they lived in the jungle. The

time passed so quickly that Jenny could hardly believe it when her mother came to pick her up. The girls squished the snakes back into a ball to use another day and washed their hands. "We didn't even have time to practice jump rope," Jenny protested as she and her mother walked to the car.

"Maybe Crystal would like to come to our house next time," said Mrs. Bingham. Just as she spoke, Crystal ran out of the house and handed Jenny the tiny clay mouse. "This is for you," she said shyly.

"Oh, thank you," Jenny said, hugging her new friend. "I'll keep it forever."

"Can I have Crystal come to my house tomorrow afternoon?" Jenny asked as they drove home.

"I have to catch up on some housecleaning tomorrow," Mrs. Bingham said. "With everyone so busy, it's hard to find time." When Jenny sighed, she smiled. "But maybe she could come on Thursday."

"Could I invite Brian, too?" Jenny asked. "He'd like to see Lady and Ginger. His mother is allergic to animals, so he can't have any."

Her mother nodded. "I think that would be all right."

"Crystal and I like to do the same things," Jenny said. "Sometimes Elaine gets grouchy, but Crystal never does."

"I'm glad to see you making lots of nice friends," Mrs. Bingham said.

Jenny leaned back in her seat, hugging herself in happiness. Next to Christmas, this had been the best day of her life.

—14—

No Surprise

"How many days until my birthday?" Jenny asked at breakfast one morning the next week.

"Birthday?" Mr. Bingham peeked over the morning paper at her. "Do you have a birthday coming up? I thought you just had one last year."

"I did," said Jenny with a giggle.

"Well, then, why would you need another one?"

"People have birthdays every year," Jenny said.

Mrs. Bingham put two slices of bread in the toaster. On Thursdays she did not go to class until late. "Does that mean you want presents and birthday cake again?" she teased.

Jenny nodded, enjoying the game.

"Did you hear that, Martin?" asked Mrs. Bingham. "She expects all that celebration again.

Why, only last year we had presents and a cake. Grandma and Grandpa even came over. And you really want to do all that again?"

Jenny stirred her spoon around her cereal bowl. "How many days?" she groaned.

Mr. Bingham suddenly glanced at his watch. "Abigail," he called. "If you don't hurry, you're going to miss breakfast."

Abigail almost flew into the kitchen. She was carrying her shoes and socks.

"What takes you so long every morning?" Mrs. Bingham scolded. "You've been in the bathroom almost an hour."

"It's not like the old days," Abigail said between bites. "I have to look perfect. Do you know how terrible it would be if my clothes clashed when I went to school?"

"You spend an hour making sure your clothes don't clash?" Mr. Bingham said in disbelief.

"Of course not, Daddy. I have to take a shower and fix my hair."

"I can get ready in five minutes," Jenny announced.

Abigail sighed. "You're going to have to pay more attention. Yesterday you wore a pink shirt and lavender pants."

"It was pretty," Jenny said.

"I thought so, too," said Mr. Bingham.

Abigail stuffed a spoonful of cereal into her mouth. "It clashed," she said determinedly. "When I grow up, I'm going to be a fashion designer, so I know about these things."

Mr. Bingham chuckled. "Then yesterday, when you were late and I found you sitting on the edge of your bed daydreaming, you were really studying ways to save the world from clashing."

"That's right," Abigail said, blushing.

"Hey," said Jenny. "No one told me how many days until my birthday."

Mrs. Bingham looked at the calender. "October twentieth will be in eight more days," she answered.

"Mrs. Archer has a crown for birthdays," Jenny said. "And the parents bring a treat for all the kids."

"Mom brought treats when I was little, too," Abigail said.

"Don't you have a birthday crown in the fourth grade?"

Abigail shook her head. "We're too big for that stuff." Her voice sounded just a little regretful.

"Well, then, I'm glad I'm only in kindergarten," said Jenny. "This will be my best birthday.

I get a crown at school and a surprise party at home." She covered her mouth. "Ooops."

"What surprise party?" Mr. and Mrs. Bingham asked at the same instant.

"The one Abigail is giving me. You know." Jenny looked from one face to another to see if they were teasing. She could tell from Abigail's look of genuine surprise that they were not. "But I heard you talking about it," she cried.

"When?" Abigail said.

"You went in the kitchen and told me not to snoop. You said *surprise.* And *present.* I heard that, too."

"You must have been snooping, then," said Abigail.

"I wasn't," Jenny said. "I was listening."

"I remember," said Mrs. Bingham. "Abigail found out that her third-grade teacher was having a baby. She and her friends wanted to give her a present."

"A baby," Jenny wailed. "I thought she was talking about me."

Abigail looked stricken. Although the girls argued, she did not really want to see Jenny unhappy. "Maybe you can have a party, even if it's not a surprise." She looked at their mother.

"I've been so busy lately, I didn't even think about a party this year," said Mrs. Bingham.

"I had one when I was in kindergarten," Abigail reminded her.

"Of course we can have a little party for your friends. Jenny, I'm sorry I didn't think of it myself." Mrs. Bingham glanced at her watch. "Look at the time. Hurry, or you girls will miss your bus."

Abigail and Jenny rushed about, collecting book bags and school papers and putting on their jackets. "We'll talk about a party tonight," said Mrs. Bingham as she handed them their lunches and kissed them good-bye.

They ran to the end of the driveway just as the bus pulled up in front of the house. Jenny slid into her seat beside Brian. "I might get to have a party," she told him. "If I do, I'll invite you."

"I hope we play Pin the Tail on the Donkey. I'm good at that," Brian said.

Elaine was back at her table. "Are your chicken pox better?" Jenny asked.

Elaine showed the two tiny scabs on her arm. "I was hardly sick at all."

"I have a surprise for you," Mrs. Archer said after the bell rang. "Next Tuesday we are going to take a little trip. We are going to a real dairy farm and find out how we get milk."

Everyone cheered, except for Harold. "I don't think I can go," he said.

"Why not?" asked Mrs. Archer.

"Because I'm going to be sick," Harold said miserably. And, as if to prove it, he promptly threw up all over his table and the floor.

In the shocked silence that followed, the only sound was Harold's quiet sobs. "I'm sorry," he gasped.

Then Mrs. Archer calmly took over. "It's all right, Harold," she soothed. "Let's go to the nurse. Jenny, would you go to the principal's office and ask them to send Mr. Mason, the custodian, to clean up? The rest of you may scoot over by my desk until he gets here."

Several of the boys and girls made gagging noises as they passed by the mess on Harold's desk. Surprisingly, Elaine, whose table was right in back of Harold's, stayed calm. "Maybe you're getting the chicken pox," she told Harold comfortingly.

Jenny hurried to the principal's office. In no time at all, Mr. Mason was there with a bucket and mop. The mess was cleaned up, Harold's mom arrived to take him home, and order was restored. But before the day was over, two more children had been sent home because of the chicken pox.

After school the next day, Mrs. Bingham took Jenny shopping for party supplies. Although Jenny still wished she was having a surprise party, it was fun to pick out paper plates, napkins, and hats to match. "Crystal would like plates with a hamster on them," she told her mother. She studied the display of party supplies. She saw clowns, ducks, dogs, turtles, and even some with Superman. But she could not find any with a hamster design.

"These kitten ones are nice," said her mother. She showed her a package with lively kittens sitting around a birthday cake.

Jenny agreed that they were nice. Her mother bought balloons and crepe paper to make the dining room festive, and prizes for the games.

"It's too late to mail out invitations," Mrs. Bingham said when they arrived home. "I'll have to call the parents." Jenny had already decided who to invite: Crystal and Brian, Elaine, Stacy, and Jake.

"I could give out invitations at school," Jenny said.

"No," Mrs. Bingham said. "That wouldn't be

fair. How would you feel if the person sitting next to you got an invitation and you didn't?"

Jenny had to admit her mother was right. "There's a lot of hard stuff like that to think about when you get big, isn't there?" she said.

"It's not so hard," said Mrs. Bingham. "You just treat other people as nicely as you'd like them to treat you. If everyone did that, we'd all be happier."

While Mrs. Bingham made the phone calls, Abigail and Jenny looked through a book of party games. "We have to play Pin the Tail on the Donkey," Jenny said. "That way Brian can win a prize. And Crystal likes to run, so maybe she'll win the peanut race."

"Everyone can come," said Mrs. Bingham. "Only one more week until the big birthday bash."

Jenny bounced in her seat with excitement. This was going to be the best birthday ever.

—15—

Birthday Secrets

Monday, Crystal was almost as excited as Jenny. "I've got you a wonderful present," she said.

"A present?" Jenny had been so busy thinking about games, she hadn't even thought about presents. "What did you get me?"

"I can't tell you, silly," Crystal answered. "But you'll love it."

"Please tell me," Jenny begged.

"My mom said I had to keep it a secret," Crystal said.

"Well, give me a little hint," Jenny said. "Is it big?"

Crystal shook her head. "I can't tell you."

"What are my two chatterboxes so excited about this morning?" Mrs. Archer asked with a smile.

"I want Crystal to tell me what she got for my birthday," Jenny said.

"I promised I wouldn't tell," said Crystal.

"If you find out what your presents are, they won't be a surprise," said Mrs. Archer.

"My mom never tells me what's in other people's presents. She knows I'll tell," said Jake.

Mrs. Archer called the other children into a circle and read a book about dairy farming.

"My aunt has some cows. She let me give the baby calf a bottle," Jake told the class.

"That sounds nice," said Mrs. Archer.

Jake shook his head. "It slobbered all over my hand."

Charlie raised his hand. "My baby sister slobbers."

"When we go to the farm tomorrow, I'm going to ask the farmer if his cows slobber," Jake announced.

Mid-morning, Mrs. Archer called Jenny and Elaine to her desk. "I've made all the arrangements for you two to go to Mrs. Lovejoy's class for reading," she said. "You will go every morning right before recess. She is waiting for you now."

Jenny looked at Crystal. "Can she come, too?"

"Not yet," said Mrs. Archer. "Don't worry. It

will only be for a few minutes each day. The rest of the time you will still be with us. And Mrs. Lovejoy is very nice."

Jenny thought about it for a minute. "Well, she has a nice name."

Mrs. Archer nodded. "I will show you where to go." Then she paused. "Are you feeling all right?"

"She's excited about her birthday," said Crystal.

"Maybe that's it," said Mrs. Archer. "Your face looks a little flushed. I hope you're not getting sick, too. I wouldn't want you to miss the trip to the dairy farm."

Mrs. Archer passed the rest of the class a dot-to-dot picture of a cow to color while she took Jenny and Elaine to Mrs. Lovejoy's classroom. "I will only be a second," she told the class before the three of them went out the door. "And while I am gone, I want Jake to be in charge."

Everyone looked amazed, Jake most of all.

"You set the class a good example," she told Jake. "When the class sees what a hard worker you are, they will work hard, too."

Jake nodded proudly. He picked up his pencil and went right to work.

"That was a good idea," Jenny said.

Mrs. Archer winked, as though they were sharing a secret. "I think so, too."

Mrs. Lovejoy turned out to be as nice as her name. She gave Jenny and Elaine each a chair and told them to sit in the circle with the other children.

"We call our reading group the Tigers," said Mrs. Lovejoy. "Does anyone want to tell Jenny and Elaine why?"

Several children raised their hands, and Mrs. Lovejoy pointed to the girl next to Jenny.

"Because we are wild about reading," said the girl, using a growly tiger voice.

"Mrs. Archer tells me you like today's book," said Mrs. Lovejoy. Jenny smiled when she saw the title: *A Kiss for Little Bear.*

"Mrs. Lovejoy is nice," said Elaine as they walked back to the kindergarten room.

"I was kind of scared, though," admitted Jenny.

"Me, too," Elaine said. Unexpectedly, she held Jenny's hand. "I was glad I had a friend with me," she said.

Jenny felt a warm glow at the words she had been waiting to hear. She would have been even happier, but her head hurt and she felt tired. It was almost time for recess, but she didn't feel much like playing.

"Maybe it's from all that reading in Mrs. Lovejoy's class," Crystal said sympathetically when the recess bell rang. "We could just sit in the shade and talk."

When they got outside, Jenny sat down under a tree, leaned back, and closed her eyes.

"Can I sit with you?" Elaine asked. "I have to keep my hair nice. After school I'm going to an audition for another commercial."

"That must be exciting," Crystal said admiringly.

Elaine sighed. "Not really. When they make commercials you have to sit in front of these big, bright lights. Then they make you do it over and over until they think it's just right."

"How come you're not chasing us?" asked Brian, peeking around the tree trunk at the girls.

"Jenny's not feeling well," Crystal told him. "I'm taking care of her."

Brian sat down beside them. "When I get big, I'd like to go to the North Pole and help Santa deliver presents. But I might drive the school bus like my grandma."

Jenny opened her eyes. "I want to be an artist when I grow up. But I might be a gymnast person on TV. I'm taking lessons."

"I wanted to take gymnastics, too," Elaine said. Then she frowned. "But my mother was afraid I'd get hurt."

"Can you stand on your hands?" Brian asked Jenny.

"Sure," said Jenny. She flipped over on her hands and walked a few steps.

Elaine and Crystal clapped. "Wow," Brian said admiringly. "That's pretty good. Maybe you *will* be on TV. I could drive you to the television station in my bus. I'll probably have a shiny red one."

Jenny rubbed her head. Standing upside down had made it hurt worse. She was glad when the bell rang and they could go back inside.

For the remainder of the morning, Jenny was very quiet. At playtime, when the rest of the class was playing Store, Jenny stayed in her seat. Mrs. Archer felt her head. "You don't seem to have any fever," she said. "But I think you might be catching something. Maybe you should lie down after school."

At last the bell rang, and the children lined up

for the bus. Jenny was surprised to see a strange woman sitting in the driver's seat.

"My grandma had a dentist appointment," Brian said.

"That's right." The woman had a friendly smile. "I will be driving you home today."

Usually Jenny sat with Brian. But he was talking to Jake, and she didn't feel like talking. She sat by herself in the back seat. She leaned her head against the window as the bus chugged along. But her head kept bumping against the glass, so she scooted herself down until she was lying in her seat. That felt a little better. Jenny closed her eyes.

"My goodness, where did you come from?" said a voice.

Jenny sat up and looked at the new driver. "From school," she said rather crossly. The new driver must not be very smart if she didn't know that. Then she noticed all of the children were gone. The bus was completely empty except for the two of them.

"What did you do with all the children?" she asked suspiciously.

"I took them all home," the driver said. "But it seems I missed someone."

"Who?" asked Jenny, peering around to see who she meant.

"I'm talking about you," the driver said with a chuckle. "You must have slept right through your stop. I imagine your parents are pretty worried."

Jenny's head hurt even worse than before, and her throat ached. Besides that, she itched all over. "I wish you would take me home," she said, almost crying. "I don't feel good, and I don't like this itchy bus at all."

The driver looked at her. "I'll call your parents right away and explain. Then we'll take you home. But I don't think it's my bus that's making you itch. Unless I miss my guess, you've got a lovely case of chicken pox."

—16—

Chicken Pox Birthday

"My teacher says that almost half the kindergarten class has chicken pox," Abigail reported the day before Jenny's birthday. "Crystal has it, and so does Brian. She says it's practically an epidemic."

"It isn't fair," said Jenny. She wanted to be brave, but she was too miserable. "I didn't get to go to the dairy farm, and now I won't even get to wear the birthday crown. And we already bought all the things for the party."

"Mama said I had chicken pox before you were born," said Abigail. "I don't even remember it."

"What was it like before I was born?" Jenny asked. She tried to picture the world without herself in it.

"I don't remember," Abigail told her. "I guess I was too little."

"What if I wake up and it's my birthday and I really didn't have chicken pox? What if this is just a dream?"

"I think about that sometimes, too," Abigail said. "But we would both have to have the same dream because I'm here, too."

"Maybe you're not really here. Maybe you're in your bed asleep," Jenny said, enjoying the game.

"Maybe you're in your bed asleep and this is my dream," Abigail said.

Jenny sighed. "No. If it was your dream, I wouldn't itch so much."

"If both of you are dreaming, maybe I should eat this ice cream," Mr. Bingham said from the door. He brought in a tray with a big bowl of chocolate ice cream for both girls.

"Maybe you're just dreaming you're bringing us some ice cream," Abigail said, laughing.

Jenny smiled. That was the only good thing about being sick. Everyone was being extra nice to her. Every afternoon when Abigail got home from school, she came in Jenny's room to keep her company.

"Would you like me to read you a story?" Abigail offered as they ate. She looked sympathetically at her sister. Jenny had chicken pox everywhere. Even though she was starting to heal, she still itched.

"I'm tired of stories," Jenny said crossly. Her bed was covered with crayons, paper, books, and games her mother had given her to keep her amused. She reached over to pet Lady. Although Lady was not usually allowed on the bed, Mrs. Bingham had made an exception, to cheer Jenny up. Even Ginger was curled on one corner of the bed, a safe distance from Lady. But nothing could take away the itching or the disappointment at missing her party.

"Can you get more chicken pox if you've already had it?" Abigail asked Mr. Bingham thoughtfully.

"No, people only get it once," he answered. "That's why we let you sit with Jenny."

Abigail still looked thoughtful. When Mr. Bingham took the dishes to the kitchen, she followed, promising to return to Jenny in a few minutes. When she came back, she looked unusually cheerful.

"Why are you so happy?" Jenny asked in a cranky voice.

"Oh, nothing," Abigail said rather mysteriously. No amount of pleading on Jenny's part would make her say any more.

That evening the whole family acted mysterious. Jenny had been allowed to come downstairs because she was feeling slightly better. But when she entered the room, everyone stopped talking and acted guilty. "Well," said Jenny indignantly. "Everybody sure is having fun when I'm sick."

The family all assured her that they were not, but still no one explained.

When her mother tucked her in that night, Jenny was cranky and miserable. "Can I go to school tomorrow for my birthday crown?"

Mrs. Bingham gave her a hug. "You're not quite well enough to go to school. You might give some of the other children chicken pox. We'll try to have a happy birthday at home."

"I'd rather go to school," Jenny said, scowling. "I hate these old chicken pox. I *want* to give them to somebody else."

The next morning Jenny bounced out of bed. She was feeling much better. Even the itching was less. Then she looked in the mirror and remembered. Today was her birthday.

She stared at her reflection to see if she looked any older. But everything seemed the same. Her new tooth was almost grown out, and the baby tooth right next to it felt a tiny bit wobbly. Her face was still covered with pock marks, although some of them had interesting scabs. She sighed. Then she padded to the bathroom to brush her teeth.

There was a paper crown on the sink. It was just like the one in Mrs. Archer's room, only fancier. This one had sparkly sequins pasted on it. There was a note card beside it.

Good morning—happy birthday.
Here's a crown for you to wear.
A breakfast feast awaits you,
So brush your teeth and comb your hair.

Smiling now, Jenny did as the note said, putting the crown on just before she left the bathroom. She admired herself in the mirror. She looked almost like a real queen. Except that real queens probably didn't have such butterflies in their stomachs.

Mrs. Bingham had fixed her favorite breakfast, French toast with lots of syrup.

"Do you like your crown?" Abigail asked. "I made it for you. Mama helped glue on all the sequins."

"It's beautiful," said Jenny, just as the doorbell rang.

"Who could that be?" Mrs. Bingham wondered out loud as she went to answer it. A minute later, she came back in the kitchen with Elaine.

"What are you doing here?" Jenny asked.

"My mother said it was all right because I already had chicken pox," said Elaine. "I had to come in the morning because I have another audition tonight." Elaine sighed. Then she smiled. "I brought you a present. You are my second best friend, aren't you?"

Elaine looked at the crown while Jenny opened her present. "No one ever made me a birthday crown," she said enviously. "I don't even get to wear one at school because my birthday is in the summer. You must have a nice family."

Jenny considered her family. Her mother was always busy, now that she was going to school. But she still found time to take care of Jenny when she was sick. Her father always made her laugh and had shown her where to find God. Abigail was sometimes grouchy. But she had played games and read to Jenny when she was sick, and she'd made her a beautiful birthday crown.

"You know what?" she told Elaine. "They are my better-than-best friends."

Elaine's present was a pretty charm bracelet with seashells on it. "I bought it in Hawaii last summer."

"It's beautiful," Jenny said. "Thank you." She was still amazed that Elaine had come.

"I thought you might like one of these, too," Elaine said. She handed her a sweatshirt. On it was a picture of Elaine holding a bottle of Sunshine Shampoo. "I have to go because my mother is waiting," said Elaine. "Happy birthday." Jenny walked her to the front door and waved as Elaine climbed into her mother's car.

"That was a nice way to start a birthday," observed Mr. Bingham, when Jenny returned to the kitchen.

Jenny admired each tiny shell on the bracelet and agreed.

"Since you are having a sick-in-bed birthday, Daddy and I decided to let you open your presents this morning," said Mrs. Bingham.

"Close your eyes," Abigail said.

Jenny waited with her eyes squeezed shut. She

heard paper rustling and a bump as packages were stacked on the coffee table.

"Hurry and open them so I can watch before I go to school," Abigail said.

Jenny tore off the wrappings as quickly as she could. There was a board game she'd been wanting, a little stuffed penguin, and a new sweater. Best of all were her purple leotard and matching tights. From Abigail was a new book. "I thought you might like that," she said. "I'll read it to you if it's too hard." Jenny looked at the title. It was called *A Very Young Gymnast*.

Jenny threw her arms around each person in the family and thanked them. But her happy feeling disappeared a minute later when she had to watch from the front room window while a still mysterious-acting Abigail climbed onto bus 23. Then, at eleven o'clock, her mother left for a class, in spite of Jenny's grumbles. "I'm sorry to leave you on your birthday," Mrs. Bingham apologized. "But you're getting better, and Daddy will be here with you."

Jenny looked at her book, and Mr. Bingham played the board game with her, so the morning went quickly. After lunch, Mr. Bingham insisted that Jenny take a nap even though it was her birthday. He did read her a story first, something deliciously scary, with a ghost and a buried treasure, but then he left her alone to sleep.

"Naps are for babies," Jenny insisted.

"And for girls who have been sick," Mr. Bingham said firmly.

"I'll never go to sleep on my birthday," Jenny shouted after him stubbornly. But her eyes nodded shut, and she was soon fast asleep.

"Wake up, sleepyhead," Mrs. Bingham said gently sometime later.

Confused, Jenny sat straight up. "I thought you were going to class."

"I did," said Mrs. Bingham. "It's four o'clock in the afternoon."

"I wasted half of my birthday," Jenny said in a grouchy voice.

"Oh, there's a lot of birthday left," Mrs. Bingham said. "Now put on your shoes and your crown and come downstairs."

Jenny hurriedly did as she was told. But when she reached the bottom step, the house was empty and quiet. "Where is everybody?" Jenny shouted.

"Surprise!" yelled voices from the kitchen. And suddenly Jenny was surrounded with the smiling faces of her family and the chicken pox-dotted faces of Brian and Crystal.

"Were you surprised?" Abigail asked, beaming at her. "It was my idea. Since we've all had the chicken pox, we couldn't make each other sick."

"We're having a chicken pox birthday," Crystal exclaimed. "Stacy and Jake haven't had it yet, so they couldn't come, but Brian and I are almost better."

The table was set with the pretty tablecloth and paper dishes, and everyone played games until it was time for cake and presents.

Crystal left the room. When she returned, she was carrying a small box. Strange scratching noises came from inside. Mr. Bingham smiled at Jenny. "You've been doing so much growing up lately that we thought you could take care of this."

Jenny carefully opened the lid. Inside was a tiny brown and white creature.

"It's one of the baby hamsters," Crystal said. "They're old enough to leave their mother now."

"It's beautiful," said Jenny. "I love it." She gave the hamster some bread and watched it stuff it into its mouth. The little pouches in its cheeks stuck out comically.

HAPPY
RTHDAY!

"I brought you some toys for the hamster," Brian said, handing Jenny a box.

"We have a nice cage for your new pet, too," said Mrs. Bingham. "What will you name it?"

Jenny looked at the hamster. It looked back with bright black eyes, as though waiting to learn its new name. Then she looked at its cheeks, still full of bread. "His name is Stuffy."

"Perfect," said Abigail approvingly.

Brian's mother picked him up after the ice cream and cake. "I liked your chicken pox party," he said as he left. "It was almost as good as Christmas."

While the rest of the Bingham family cleaned up the table, Crystal and Jenny took Stuffy to Jenny's room to play.

"This is the best present I ever had," Jenny said. She smiled at Crystal and impulsively gave her a hug. "Would you like to be my best friend?"

Crystal hugged her back and giggled. "Of course, silly. I already am."